Dipika placed a hand o good thing the call cam us take this a bit slow, understand his impatience as her own body craved his touch, his lovemaking, as desperately as a man seeking water in the middle of the desert.

He turned sideways to glance at her, the tautness leaving his body when he noticed her beautiful face and imploring eyes. "Okay, I'm not going to ask again, not until you beg me to love you."

She gave him a wide smile, pulling his face down for a kiss. "You're the best."

"If you say so," he growled before kissing her deeply. When they finally came up for air, he said, "I hope that keeps you awake the whole night."

She laughed softly, hugging him. "It's not what you did to me that is going to keep me awake. But what you didn't do to me."

"Serve you right."

She reached a hand and placed it over his fly, stroking down the length of his manhood, her eyebrow up in query as she gave him a teasing glance. "You going to sleep well tonight?"

Mudit groaned long and loud, wanting to protest, but liking her touch too much. "You're killing me, Dippy."

ABOUT THE AUTHOR

Sundari Venkatraman is an Indie Author who has 71 books to her credit. These books have consistently featured in the Top 100 Bestseller Lists on Amazon Kindle, in both romance as well as Asian Drama categories. Her latest hot romances have all been on #1 Bestseller slot in Amazon India for over a month.

LIBRA'S FLAME is a hot romance novel and the fifth book in the Written in the Stars series. It can also be read as a standalone novel. This kindle book remained in the #1 Bestseller position on Amazon India for three months after its release.

Even as a child, Sundari absolutely loved the 'lived happily ever after' syndrome and she grew up on a steady diet of fairy tales, Phantom comics, and Mandrake comics. It was always about good triumphing over evil and a happy ending after the protagonists surmounted all unexpected obstacles.

Once she entered her teens, Sundari switched her loyalties from fairy tales to Mills & Boon. While she loved reading both, she kept visualising what would have happened if there were similar situations happening in India; to local heroes and heroines. And of course, the joy of vanquishing the ubiquitous evil villains! Her imagination soared and she happily ensconced herself in a rosy romantic cocoon for many years.

Then came the writing—a true bolt from the blue! And Sundari Venkatraman has never looked back.

Books by Sundari Venkatraman

Standalone novels
The Malhotra Bride
Meghna
The Madras Affair
An Autograph for Anjali
Twin Torment
Finding Anya
Mr. Perfect
Man Friday
Her Prince Charming
Love in Agartha
Arjun's Penance
The Floundering Author
Ryan Finds a Bride
Tinder Loving Care
Shaan Gets Hitched
For Better or For Worse
Love… No Conditions Asked

Collection of shorts
Matches Made in Heaven
Tales of Sunshine

Marriages Made in India Series
#1 The Runaway Bridegroom
#2 Her Smitten Husband
#3 His Drunken Wife
#4 Her Secret Husband
#5 The Casanova's Wife
#6 Her Bohemian Husband

The Bansal Legacy Trilogy
#1 Simha International
#2 Rose Garden International
#3 Maharaja International

The Thakore Royals Trilogy
#1 The Marriage Predicament
#2 Tied in Knots
#3 The Wooing of the Shrew

The Groom Series Trilogy
#1 Groomnapped
#2 Gobsmacked
#3 Grounded

Arora Iyers Trilogy
#1 Once Bitten Twice Lucky
#2 Heartthrob
#3 Call of the Heart

Written in the Stars Series
#1 Scorpio Superstar
#2 Leo's Desire
#3 Taurus Temptation
#4 Virgo's Krush
#5 Libra's Flame
#6 Aquarius Rebel

Dashavatar (Indian Mythology)
MATSYA: The First Avatar
KURMA: The Second Avatar
VARAHA: The Third Avatar
NARASIMHA: The Fourth Avatar
VAMANA: The Fifth Avatar
PARASHURAMA: The Sixth Avatar

The Prince Series (Historical Romance)
#1 The Banished Prince
#2 The Crown Prince

The Princess Series (Historical Romance)
#1 The Passionate Princess
#2 The Rebel Princess

The Writer's Toolkit (Non-fiction)
Publishing Your Book on Amazon KDP

Bollywood Bros Trilogy
#1 Sing For Me
#2 Dance With Me
#3 Lights, Camera, Action!

Romantic Shorts Series
#1 Chahti Hoon Tumhe
#2 Beauty is but Skin Deep
#3 Madeinheaven.com
#4 An Arranged Match
#5 The Reluctant Bride
#6 Shweta ka Swayamvar
#7 Pappa's Girl
#8 Red Rose Dating Agency
#9 Rahat Mili
#10 Reema's Matchmakers
#11 The Matchmaker's Dream

LIBRA'S FLAME

WRITTEN IN THE STARS
BOOK 5

A romance novel by
SUNDARI VENKATRAMAN

*Love,
Sundari*

FLAMING SUN

First Published by Flaming Sun 2025
Printed & Distributed by Notion Press
Copyright © Sundari Venkatraman 2025
All Rights Reserved.

ISBN 979-8-89699-060-4

All rights reserved. No part of this publication may be reproduced, stored in a retrieval system, or transmitted, in any form or by any means, (electronic, mechanical, photocopying, recording or otherwise) without the prior permission of the author-publisher.

Sundari Venkatraman asserts the moral right to be identified as the author & publisher of this book.

This is a work of fiction and any resemblance to real persons, living or dead, is purely coincidental.

This book is sold subject to the condition that it shall not, by way of trade or otherwise, be lent, hired out, or otherwise circulated without the publisher's prior consent in any form of binding or cover other than that in which it is published and without a similar condition including this condition being imposed on the subsequent purchaser.

Editor: The Book Club Editorial Panel
Beta Read by: Lakshmi Ranganathan
Cover Illustration: Vivek Chandanshiv

Essentially, Gemini and Libra are wonderfully compatible, possessing many virtues (as well as vices) in common. They tend to respect each other's mentality, privacy, and freedom of thought and speech—normally. Romance will eternally be more important to both Gemini and Libra than sex. This attitude will predominate and suffuse their intimacy with a beauty all its own.

- LINDA GOODMAN

ACKNOWLEDGEMENT

A special thanks to JENI THAKKAR IYER for helping me with the Gujarati phrases. While she insists it was no big deal for her, it was of immense help to me, as I don't know Gujarati to save my life. Thank you so much Jeni. You are the best!

1

Mudit Trivedi lifted his head to check out the fair ground in Vile Parle which was flooded with revellers who were there to celebrate the Navratri festival by dancing the *garba* and *dandiya*, whichever took their fancy. Belonging to a Gujarati family, he was used to attending the festivities year after year, at least during the long weekends. Which meant that he was there on at least three to five nights.

It had all begun to pall! And he was not even sure from when. But then, Tanvi Desai, his girlfriend of six months, was keen they should attend, that too, on all the nine days. He believed that if she had her way, Mudit would be dancing and partying on all three hundred and sixty-five days of the year. He shook his head to clear it of negative thoughts. They both liked each other and the chemistry was good. No way was he going to spoil it all with his judgemental thinking. But then, Mudit was rather cynical at thirty-two, and could sense somewhere deep down that his relationship with Tanvi was going south.

He grimaced as he searched for the petite Tanvi, the top of whose head barely reached his shoulder. Where was she?

Colours swirled in front of his eyes, even as the music rose to a crescendo. But no sight nor sound of Ms. Desai. He had a good mind to walk away from it all! Phew! When was the last time he had simply sat back in his home library, rifling through an interesting book, while enjoying a bottle of beer? Or maybe even a glass of wine?

He simply couldn't recall! Which only made him all the more miffed. He dug into the side pocket of his black *kurta* only for the flap of his ink blue, heavily embroidered waistcoat to get in the way. Frowning heavily, he pushed it away to reach for his cell phone, clicking it open to call Tanvi.

"Hey Handsome!" An older woman placed her hand on his elbow to catch his attention.

What the fuck! Mudit glared at the woman who was smiling at him enticingly, fluttering her false eyelashes invitingly.

"Buzz off!" he snarled at her before turning the other way as he waited for Tanvi to pick up his call. But then, he was not sure if she would hear the ring, not with the noise around them. It was not only the music, but everyone talking above the sound, all at once. He impatiently waited for Tanvi to take his call, only in vain.

Where the hell was she? He looked this way and that, his eyes falling on the food stalls, zeroing in on a woman who was wearing a heavily embroidered *gaghra choli*, in black and blue. Her thick hair was piled into an unruly knot at the crown of her head. Unruly, because a number of strands were dancing all around her beautifully made-up face. Without even realising what he was doing, he forgot all about Tanvi and began walking towards the stranger, his feet appearing to have a mind of their own.

"Kabir!" Dipika Sanyal went on her knees beside her little nephew who was so cute in his black *churidar kurta* and royal blue waistcoat. He seemed to have lost his embroidered cap though, his silky hair tousled delightfully.

Kabir lifted his arms to his paternal aunt, a winning smile on his charming little face. "Dippy Aunty," he greeted her enthusiastically, giving her a wet kiss on her cheek.

Dipika laughed softly as she lifted him up in her arms before standing up. "Where are your Mamma and Dada?" she asked, laughing some more. While the Sanyals all lived in the same house, Dipika had come to the grounds directly from a client meeting while her brother Krish, his wife Sanjana and Baby Kabir had all come from home.

Kabir cackled as if she had cracked a funny joke before turning to point a little finger towards the dancing couple. "There!"

It was only after seeing Krish and Sanjana, did Dipika notice Lata, Kabir's nanny, standing barely a couple of feet away from where he had been. Phew! "Lata!"

"Dipika *di*," smiled the younger woman, happy to see Kabir's aunt.

"You go on and have some fun. I'll take care of Kabir."

An eager light came into Lata's eyes as she turned around to stare at the revellers. How she would love to dance along with them! "But…"

"Just go and have fun." Dipika pushed the younger woman towards the crowd.

Lata waved at Kabir before joining the circle of people who were dancing the *garba,* excited to participate in the levity.

"Do you want to dance?" asked Dipika, pushing the lock of hair which had fallen on Kabir's forehead.

"Kabir hungry," declared the child, giving her a toothy smile.

"Hahaha! Let us get you something to eat." She bent down to place him on the ground, taking his hand in hers before turning towards the line of food stalls.

"Hey! Haven't me met before?" Mudit was surprised to find himself breathless as he stood close to the young woman who held a little boy firmly by the hand. He did not give a damn that the pick-up line was an old one and probably worn to shreds. After all, she was the most beautiful woman he had ever set his eyes on.

Dipika stopped in her tracks to look up at the stranger who seemed to have appeared from nowhere. A small frown of concentration pleated her forehead while she studied him. *I would have never forgotten his face, not if I have seen it before!* In that case, it was definitely a pick-up line, and it was anything but original. A fist on one slender hip, she tilted her head to one side as she smiled up at him. "I'm sure you remember my name. Go on, tell me." Her sherry brown eyes danced with mischief as she stared up into his handsome face. She ignored the fact that her heart had picked up speed at the stranger's proximity, to beat at double pace.

"That's the problem, *yaar*. It's right here, but…" He shook his head, pointing at his own throat. He gave her a charming smile which lit up his whole face and made him even more attractive.

A hand at her own throat as if to calm down the rapid pulse beating there, Dipika laughed softly, shaking her head. "Excuse me. Kabir is hungry and we are going to eat something at the stalls."

"Yes. I want chicken burger," said Kabir firmly, smiling up at the stranger.

Mudit went down on his knees to meet Kabir at eye level. "Hello Kabir. I'm Mudit. How do you do?"

Kabir gave the stranger a winning smile. "Hello Mudit!"

Dipika glared at the top of Mudit's head before speaking to her nephew. "Mudit Uncle."

Kabir gave her a sage nod. "Mudit Uncle," he parroted her words.

"Good boy." She ruffled Kabir's head as she smiled down at him.

Mudit tilted his face towards her, his deep grey eyes clinging to hers as he invited her touch.

Dipika's eyes went wide as she gave him a startled glance. Talk about being forward! "Bye Mudit!" she said, stepping back to walk around the man who was still on his knees.

"I didn't get your name?" he called out to her retreating back.

She turned to give him a mock glare and a thumbs down before striding ahead.

"Dippy Aunty." Kabir turned to call out to his new friend before falling into step with his aunt.

A wide smile stretched Mudit's lips as he stared after the two. So! She, Dippy, was not Kabir's mother, but his aunt. Was he glad to know that!

"Here you are!" Tanvi slid a hand into the crook of his elbow. "I've been looking for you all over the place."

He turned around to stare at his girlfriend—ex, to be precise—his eyes blank as if he could not recognise the woman who was clinging to his side. But then, he was so enamoured with Dippy that the rest of the female population seemed to have become non-existent.

"Do you wanna dance? That's my favourite song they are playing." Without waiting for his answer, she took his hand in hers and dragged him towards the dancers, or at least tried to.

Mudit dug his feet in, refusing to move. "Listen, Tanvi. I've had enough. Let's leave."

"What?" She screeched as she turned to glare at him. "It's not even ten yet. How can you talk of leaving?"

"I just realised I have an urgent meeting tomorrow, first thing in the morning." Mudit lied through his teeth. He did not care if Tanvi wanted to leave or not. He had had enough.

"But tomorrow is Saturday!" Tanvi screeched at him; her face turning red with anger as she glared up into his face. "Who works during the weekend?"

"I do," he insisted stubbornly, his fists on his hips as he glared right back at her. Well, that was at least true, that he worked on Saturdays; which was only because he enjoyed what he did.

Tanvi was thoroughly confused. Where had the gentle giant she had known for over six months disappeared to? The man in front of her was anything but affable. But then, it did not strike her that Mudit was a Gemini and had two personalities, each one entirely different from the other. All this long, she had only seen the fun, friendly and good-natured side of him. "But... but we agreed to stay until at least midnight." Actually, if it had been in Tanvi's hands, she would have insisted they remain at the venue much later than that.

He tilted his head to look down his sharp nose at her, his eyes shut in a half-slit, and his arms folded across his massive chest. "I don't recall doing any such thing," he disagreed, a mutinous thrust to his square chin.

Maybe he was right. After all, she had never asked him, but had simply presumed they would stay back until the early hours of the morning. Which was exactly what they had done over the last few days. Why the hell was he taking an objection today? Equally belligerent, she placed her fists on her slender hips to look up at him, thoroughly miffed when she had to tilt her head a long way back. "Does it matter now? The programme is on until late. You knew that when we purchased the tickets. I..."

He lifted a hand to stop her mid-sentence, totally fed up by now. "Do you know people here? Your relatives or friends, maybe?"

"Duh! Of course, I do. I..."

"Perfect! I'm sure someone will give you a lift back home. Bye!" He did an about turn and walked away from her, his mind completely on Dippy as he ignored the shrieking Tanvi as she rushed behind him, flapping her arms.

She stopped after a few steps as he was walking too fast for her to catch up. She would show him tomorrow, swore Tanvi to herself. *I'll show him that he cannot manipulate me like this.*

What Tanvi did not realise was that Mudit had already moved on. And there was not much she could do as he had made no promises. Just a few dates did not constitute permanency, did they?

Mudit could not stop thinking about Dipika as he drove his car out of the parking area, glad to be leaving. If they stayed a couple of hours longer, getting the car out would have been a horrible experience as there were at least four hundred vehicles of various shapes and sizes parked to one side of the ground. It must be a nightmare doing this over nine days. The long weekends were the worst and today being Friday, he sure had had a lucky escape, thanks to Dippy.

He smiled to himself when he thought of the lovely lady, wondering if he would see her again. Would she be there if he went back to the *dandiya* grounds the next evening? He grimaced. It would be too much of an effort to do that; and he did not want to get caught with Tanvi again. Thinking about it, he could not really understand what he had seen in her all this long. All Tanvi wanted to do in life was to have fun. It had not mattered to him in the beginning. It was only later, during their dinner dates, that he realised they had nothing in common. She hated the printed word, while he read every day. She liked to party on all three hundred and sixty-five days of the year, while he went to parties on maybe ten days in a year, preferring to hang out with like-minded friends on some weekends. He enjoyed travelling solo, or maybe with a single partner—though he was yet to find someone who would enjoy the same—while Tanvi wanted to always be surrounded by a crowd of friends, both male and female. They all seemed so young, making him feel ancient. While their giggles drove him crazy.

Was he ready to brave it back to the *dandiya* grounds for Dippy's sake? And what was the chance that she would be there?

It had been a mistake not to insist on taking her phone number. He should have hung out for a bit longer maybe. Tch! Instead of running away from the venue in fear of Tanvi.

Damn!

As for Dipika, she was smiling throughout the evening whenever she thought of the hunk who had flirted with her. He was not only stunningly attractive, but appeared intelligent too. And that was a real turn on for her. The only time she had had a boyfriend was almost a decade ago. And the affair had lasted for less than three weeks. She realised that Vijay had been simply too immature for her taste. The extent of his conversation had been all about Vijay—his wants, his needs, and his wishes. It had been a relief to be rid of the man. And after that, she had thrown herself into her work and was too happy to remain single.

Meeting Mudit—though she could not really call it a meeting *per se*—had set her thinking of him, even making her smile a lot. And did it matter that she caught sight of a woman clinging to his arm when she turned around to check him out for the last time? Not really, as it was she who was holding his arm and not the other way round.

Will I meet him again? She could not help but feel disappointed when she did not catch sight of the handsome Mudit until the time the Sanyals left the grounds around midnight.

Dipika stretched her arms wide even as she yawned, trying to wrap her mind around the elusive dream which hovered at the edge of her conscious mind, refusing to come to the surface. It was not yet seven in the morning, but it was already late for one who was used to waking up at six or earlier. But it had been almost one am when Dipika, her brother Krish, his wife Sanjana, their little son Kabir and his nanny, Lata, had returned home from the *dandiya raas* programme they had been to.

Thinking of which brought back the elusive memory of her dream to the forefront of her conscious mind. It was that tall and charismatic stranger she had met at the dance grounds. Mudit! Even while she had laughed at his obvious pick-up line, she had found herself turning back to check him out, stopping every few steps she had taken with her nephew towards the food stall.

Mudit's personality was striking, even more than his handsome looks. And his smile had been mesmerising when he had looked into her eyes with his deep grey ones which shone with intelligence.

What the hell was she doing dreaming about him? First of all, there had been that woman standing beside him. Whether it was she clinging to him, or the other way round, there was a strong possibility that they were a couple. And also there was the fact that he was a stranger. What were the chances of her meeting him once again in the next twenty-nine years?

She jumped out of her bed as if scalded, a deep frown drawing her well-shaped eyebrows together as she went into the bathroom. It was still not too late to go for a jog, she decided, as she looked critically at her own face in the mirror while brushing her teeth.

Dragging on a pair of cotton shorts and a sleeveless vest, she tied her long, thick, and curly hair back with a bandana to make sure the strands didn't fall over her forehead and consequently into her eyes. Pulling on a pair of socks and sneakers over her narrow feet, tucking her smart phone into a hip pocket, plugging her earbuds into her ears before switching on the songs from her favourite playlist on YouTube Music, Dipika stepped out of the front door, shutting it firmly behind her.

She took deep breaths as she stretched, warming up before taking off at a fast walk down the lane, and on towards Versova beach. She jogged beside the water's edge, humming along with a fast Bollywood number, a smile on her face.

"Hey, we meet again." Mudit, who was running along the shore from the opposite direction, stopped next to the woman—Dippy—he had met the earlier evening. This was a pleasant coincidence indeed. He jogged this way every day of the week, but had never come across her before today. He was not to know that Dipika was late today by about an hour. She usually went jogging at around six am and probably was back home even before he stepped out on the beach.

Dipika stopped in her tracks when she noticed a man waving his hand in front of her face. She pulled her earbuds out to hear the tail end of his sentence even as she frowned up at Mudit, unable to believe her eyes. He appeared a tad too cheerful this early in the morning. Being a Libra, she generally had a sunny nature; but right now, she was pretty miffed with him, all because he was obviously attached to another woman. Her hands fisted on her slender hips, she looked up at him unsmilingly.

"Dippy, right? Good morning," Mudit called out cheerfully, offering his hand for a shake.

Ignoring his outstretched hand, Dipika scowled at him some more. "Morning," she offered, still without a smile.

"Hey, are you upset about something?" he asked, cottoning on to the fact that she was irritated.

She shrugged. *"Nahi toh?* If you will excuse me, I need to go." She began to jog in earnest, forgetting to plug her ears.

"No issues. This direction works for me too," he said, falling right into step beside her.

Dipika turned to her left and glared at the man who had matched his longer strides to her shorter ones, regretting it immediately when she noticed his muscular bare legs, tanned evenly all over. Phew! Her temper spiking, she snarled, "Why don't you leave me alone?"

He turned around to jog backwards, a charismatic grin stretching his sexy mouth, unwittingly drawing her gaze to it. "Come on, Dippy. I just want to get to know you. What's the harm in that?"

"What if you are a serial killer?" she muttered under her breath as she increased her pace.

"What?!" He stopped in his tracks to burst out laughing. He reached over to take her elbow and stopped her from continuing on her way. "Do you need some references maybe?" he asked, a serious note entering his voice.

What was with the man? Why wouldn't he leave her alone? It was not as if he did not have a girlfriend. And the worst part of it was that she did not want him to leave her alone. Dipika was attracted to him like... like she had never been enamoured with another man, ever before in her life. And well, her baby nephew Kabir had given the stranger a wide smile, which was a character certificate in itself. Children tended to sense if someone was not nice. She stared at Mudit's striking face, not knowing how to deal with the situation. She, twenty-nine-year-old Dipika Sanyal, successful business woman who headed a modelling agency, beautiful and sought after by many eligible young men, was speechless for the first time in her life. She looked into his dancing grey eyes, feeling totally helpless as she felt her lungs fight for the breath which seemed to have been sucked out right from within her being.

"Dippy..." Mudit framed her face in his hands, feeling himself drowning in the glowing brown of her gaze which shone so brightly even as the sunlight shimmered over the waves which in turn threw the light over her beautiful face. Unable to stop himself, he pressed his mouth to hers, stroking his tongue over her luscious lips, sucking on them gently before thrusting his tongue into her mouth.

With a long-drawn-out sigh, she protested, "That's not really my name..." against his lips, before returning his kiss eagerly, her hands clinging to his wide shoulders even as her legs turned to jelly. If it had not been for him holding her firmly, his large hands spanning her small waist, she might have found herself floating in deep water, literally.

Lifting his mouth from hers when his lungs were fit to bursting, Mudit drew deep breaths even as he gazed down at her face. "What is your name?" he asked, speaking right into her ear as he brushed his lips over the curve, finding it too irresistible.

"Dipika Sanyal."

He moved away to stare down at her face, his eyebrows gathering together in a small frown of concentration. "Any relation to Krish Sanyal?"

An expression of wonder crossed her face. Did this mean that Mudit knew her brother? "I'm Krish's sister."

"Aah!" He snapped his fingers. "Why didn't I guess before? The little guy I met yesterday, Kabir... he is Krish's son, right?"

She gave him a nod, a soft smile stretching her lips. "You didn't recognise him?" she asked, her eyes laughing up at him.

Mudit laughed outright, shrugging. "I'm not really surprised. The last I saw Kabir was when he was barely three months old."

Dipika stared at Mudit curiously. "You attended Krish's wedding then?" How the hell had she missed him?

Mudit shook his head. "I didn't. I was travelling on work. By the way, I am with Mathur Industries. I…"

"Arjun Mathur." Speak of the world being a small place!

Mudit gave a brief nod. "You know him, of course."

"Of course. He's Krish's best friend."

He nodded again. "Mine too." It was just a statement of fact, and no more.

Dipika lifted an eyebrow at him, as if to ask how the two men—Mudit and Arjun—knew each other.

Taking her hand in his, he drew her along with him as they continued to walk on the beach. "My grandfather, Shiamak Trivedi, used to run the company soon after Arjun's father died. That was when Arjun was still studying abroad. I joined the company when my grandfather retired and Arjun took over as the CEO."

She listened to him avidly, keen to know everything about him. For the moment, she had forgotten all about the young woman clinging to Mudit's arm the earlier evening at the *dandiya* grounds.

"I handle the finance department." Actually, he was on the board of directors of the company, as the Finance Director.

She nodded again, walking along with him, not aware of where they were going, until Mudit opened the gate to a bungalow twenty minutes later. Stopping in her tracks, she turned to ask him, "Is this your place?"

"Yes."

"This is where I take my leave then," she said, her lips drooping with disappointment. She would have loved to spend more time with him.

"Not before having a cup of coffee. Come on, Dipika!" he insisted, his gruff baritone at its most persuasive.

She looked down at herself, grimacing. While her brief cotton shorts were perfect attire for jogging along the beach, they were not exactly what she wanted to be dressed in while meeting a Gujarati family first thing in the morning. "I don't think so. Your family…"

"…consists only of I, me, and myself," he said, giving her a broad grin.

Dipika stared at him, startled. And she did not miss the dejection lurking at the very back of his eyes. Did he miss his family? Where were they? "Oh! You live alone?"

He shrugged, taking her hand in his to drag her along with him to the front door. "Yes. This used to be my grandfather's house. I moved in with him when I was twelve years old." His father had sent him away as Mudit had been a difficult child to manage, not when he had the tendency to lead all his three younger siblings—two brothers and one sister—into a load of mischief. When Mudit's grandfather, Shiamak, had offered to take the twelve-year-old in, his father had jumped at the chance and sent him away. There was also another reason for it. Chandulal, Mudit's father, had been doing badly financially, and had been relieved of the pressure when one child had been sent away to be taken care off by Shiamak Trivedi. While Mudit had loved his grandfather more than anyone else in the world, he had been terribly hurt by his father's decision. He had also felt betrayed when his mother did not raise an objection to him being thrown out of their family home. Well, that was how it had appeared to little Mudit, as if he was being discarded by his own family.

His grandfather had died three years ago, and the thirty-two-year-old Mudit still missed the old man as one would miss a limb. As for his parents and siblings, he communicated with them sporadically, sending them money whenever they were in need. But there was no love lost between him and his immediate family.

Dipika was curious about his parents. But she refrained from asking anything as they stepped into the main hall of his home. It was grand, she thought and was nothing like a bachelor pad. It was beautifully decorated with hand woven rugs and comfortable sofas, both single and double, with a number of cushions piled over them in jewel colours. Small tables were set at strategic corners, a couple of them containing ceramic vases overflowing with freshly cut roses and asters in soft shades of pink, peach and red interspersed with white lilies.

Wow!

The walls shone brightly with pretty water colours, painted by local artists, bringing to life scenes from everyday life from both Mumbai and Gujarat.

"You have a beautiful house," she said, turning to smile at Mudit.

"I'm glad you think so." He dipped his head in a small nod as he avidly studied her animated face. "It is all thanks to Kishorilal, who has been managing this house from even before the time I came to live here."

An older man, probably around fifty years of age, stepped from one of the doorways at the back of the hall. "Good morning, Mudit *baba*. Where will you have your coffee?"

"Good morning, Kishore Uncle. As you can see, I have a guest today. This is Dipika Sanyal, a friend. And Dipika, this is Kishorilal. I live an extremely comfortable life at home thanks to Kishore Uncle."

Kishorilal smiled at Dipika, folding his hands in a greeting. "Welcome, ma'am."

"*Namaste* Kishore Uncle." Dipika took the cue from Mudit and greeted the older man with the respect he was due. "You must call me Dipika and not ma'am."

Kishorilal gave her a nod of agreement.

"Will you please send two coffees to the library?" Mudit instructed the older man before taking Dipika's hand and drawing her towards the third door, also at the back of the hall.

"Whoa!" Dipika's eyes grew round with wonder as she looked around her. It felt as if she had stepped straight into Aladdin's cave, only the treasure she found here was all in the guise of books. Three of the walls were covered by shelves overflowing with books of all kinds, while the fourth wall was a sheet of glass, looking out into a garden full of trees and flowering shrubs. *Was this how heaven would appear?*

Mudit grinned at her, proud as a peacock. While it was his grandfather who had set up the library in the first place, he, Mudit, had added most of the books to it. He loved to read into the early hours of the morning, and did not really bother what the book's genre was, so far as it was well written. Along with fiction, there were also a number of biographies and travelogues in the library's collection. "From the delight on your face,

I presume you read?" he asked, unable to remove his gaze from her face as she turned this way and that to check out the shelves.

"You presume right," she said, walking towards the left end of the shelves, feeling like Alice in Wonderland. She completely forgot all about her host as she ran her forefinger over the spines of the varied titles, smiling each time she found a familiar one.

His hands tucked into the pockets of his running shorts, Mudit watched her with his intense grey eyes, not really sure if he should feel happy that she was excited about his collection of books, or miffed that she seemed to be completely unaware of him. As for himself, Mudit was totally conscious of Dipika, studying her profile avidly. It was an effort not to touch her silky soft cheek or her rosy lips. He was not sure if the kiss had been a mistake. Now that he had tasted her, he realised he only wanted more. And they did not even know each other well.

It was a wonder that she had not slapped him outright when he had taken the liberty to fuse his mouth to hers. His hands itched to gather her once again into his arms and make love to every delicious inch of her.

Feeling the intense heat of his gaze, Dipika suddenly turned around to look at him, a shapely eyebrow lifting in inquiry. "What?" she asked, her voice dry as she forced the word out from her choking throat. For the past few minutes, she had completely forgotten that she was a guest in Mudit's home, and she was visiting him for the first time. Moreover, he was a stranger. Well, he knew her brother well, and he worked with Arjun Mathur, who was a friend. But even then, she did not really know him.

Soft colour flooded her face when she recalled the kiss she had shared with him earlier. Dipika was amazed at herself. It was not at all like her to allow a veritable stranger to kiss her. In fact, she had never been kissed by any man before, not the way Mudit had kissed her, so deeply, exploring her mouth as if his life had depended on it.

Mudit took a step closer, pulling his hands out of his pockets, only to stop in his tracks when a maid knocked on the library door before entering with a loaded tray in her hands. He turned to the left to relieve the maid of the heavy tray, giving her a dismissing nod.

Dipika stared at him, fascinated. He appeared to be nothing short of royalty, his nod commanding the maid to do his bidding without bothering to utter a single word.

"Come," he invited Dipika, placing the tray on the large work desk which took up pride of place in the middle of the rectangular room. He pointed to one of the twin chairs which were placed in front of the desk; parking his neat butt on the corner of the desk once she was seated. He poured the coffee into two mugs before handing one to her, smiling when her fingers came in contact with his when she took the mug from him. "Have some *khakra*," he suggested, lifting a plateful of *methi khakra* and offering it to her.

Dipika scrunched up her nose at him even as she shook her head, the curly strands of her hair bouncing on her shoulders, catching the sunlight streaming through the east facing windows. "It's too early in the morning for me to eat anything."

"Mmm." Mudit broke off a piece and munched on it as he continued to study her with his deep grey eyes. She was indeed a sight for sore eyes and he was happy to have her in his home; in his favourite room. No, he was not going to think of her in his bedroom. It was too early in the day, and in their relationship, for that matter. And well, he had never brought a woman home before today, not when his grandfather had been alive; not after he had passed on. "So, when do you have breakfast?" he asked conversationally, watching her lips as she sipped on her coffee.

She shrugged. "I suppose I'm not really a breakfast person." She screwed up her eyes as if she needed to think hard before coming up with the next sentence. "More the brunch or lunch kind." She ate when she felt hungry, many a time forgetting a meal unless prodded by someone. It was either her brother's wife Sanjana, who also happened to be Dipika's executive assistant; or Narasimha, the cook, who called her attention towards food. A surprising trait for a Libra woman. Generally, Libras loved food. While Dipika also enjoyed food, she was pretty absent-minded regarding meals, while dinner was her favourite meal of the day.

"I'll remember that," he promised, placing his empty coffee mug on the tray. "I love to eat, all the time, I suppose." He gave her an unapologetic grin.

Did he really? Dipika gave him a surprised glance as she could not notice an ounce of spare flesh on his tall and muscular frame. Forgetting herself, she continued to study him all the way from the top of his sleek black head to his broad, sock-clad feet.

"Will I do?" he asked, tongue firmly tucked in his cheek, his grey eyes dancing with mischief. While he teased, he could not help but feel pleased by her obvious interest in his physique.

"Eh?" She lifted her startled brown gaze up to his twinkling grey one, not having caught his meaning. Noticing the expression in his face, a slow grin split her own as she gave him a small nod. "I suppose."

"Tch tch!" He shook his head, taking her hands in his to pull her to her feet before drawing her between his well-muscled thighs. Placing her hands on his manly shoulders, he wrapped his own around her slender waist. "I can span your waist with my hands." He stated the obvious as he did just that, his fingers splayed at her lower back even as the tips of his thumbs met against her navel.

Dipika shivered in his hold, her hands tightening on his shoulders as she gripped him firmly, doing her best not to fall against his chest and burying her face into the crook of his shoulder. Which was exactly what she wanted to do!

"Dippy!" He leaned forward to nuzzle her neck, brushing his lips over the leaping pulse.

Drawing a deep breath to nudge awake her sluggish brain, she placed her hands firmly on his chest before moving away from his tempting body. "I need to go."

"Give me a minute," he whispered, tracing a path up to her jaw, his manly lips playing havoc with her nerves. He caught her ear lobe between his teeth, nibbling on it gently, not really surprised when his manhood sprang to attention. "You taste so damn good."

Inadvertently tilting her head to accommodate him, she sighed ecstatically, thrilled to feel his damp tongue stroking the said lobe once he was done with the love bites. Her breasts felt heavy as they pressed to his chest, the nipples turning pebble hard as they rubbed against his granite hard body. "Do you gym regularly?" The words simply popped out of her mouth as she watched in morbid fascination when her hands travelled from his shoulders down his arms to caress his hefty biceps. He was sleek and well-muscled without appearing beefy. And all she wanted to do was burrow into him and forget the rest of the world.

"Eh?" Mudit moved back a tiny inch to look down at her flushed face, a small frown pleating his forehead as if he had to strain hard to understand her words. Which was the truth as he had been lost in her eager response to his tactile exploration. Taking a deep breath to centre himself, he answered her. "I go swimming almost every day. And of course, jogging too."

"You swim?" she asked, giving him a wide-eyed glance as if it was an uncommon feat. "Where? How do you find the time for it?"

He laughed softly. "I have a swimming pool, right here, behind my house. I swim kind of late at night, once I get back from work."

"Aren't you lucky?!" There was a trace of envy in her voice as she continued to gaze into his eyes. What a gorgeous shade of grey they were! Like the turbulent Arabian Sea on a rainy morning; with thick eyebrows above them. Coming to think of it, he had expressive eyebrows. Imagine that! While his nose reminded her of the hawk which sometimes flew out to the mango tree in her compound; prominent and sharp with a slight downward curve to the tip. His cheeks were lean, coated with an overnight beard while his chin was square. But it was his lips which drew her gaze repeatedly, the thin upper one and thick lower one. On anyone else, they might have appeared feminine in their pinkness, but not on him. "Don't you smoke?" she asked out of the blue, following her own line of thought.

"Eh?" He gave her a surprised glance. "How did you guess?"

Colour flared on her cheeks as she looked up into his eyes before bringing her gaze down to his mouth. "Er... your lips..." She stopped, not sure of how to continue with the conversation which seemed to have completely got out of her control.

"What about my lips?" he asked, his voice a hoarse whisper now as he leaned forward to touch his forehead to hers. "You like them?" he asked, giving her a naughty grin as he flirted outrageously with her.

"I need to get back home. It must be late... I..."

"No way. Not when the conversation just got interesting," he protested, holding her within the circle of his arms. While his hold was loose, he made sure there was no way she could escape. "What about my lips?" he repeated.

"Uff!" She tried to push him away, only to realise that her hands had a mind of their own as they traced the contours of his wide chest, revelling in the muscular structure. "Let me go, Mudit."

"In a moment; once you answer my question."

She gazed up at him, unable to tear her gaze away from his. "I was just curious that your lips weren't dark; unlike those men who smoke."

"So! You study men's lips, do you?"

Temper flared in Dipika's eyes, making the sherry brown colour shimmer as she glared at him. She fisted her right hand and hit him on his chest, hard too.

"Ouch!" he protested, taking her fist in his left hand, and held it firmly, not really surprised when he felt her punch him with her left fist. "Aren't you a she-cat! Stop it, woman. You're hurting me."

"Good! You must admit you asked for it."

He grimaced, taking her left fist in his right hand, now holding both her fists with ease. "I suppose I did. Will it help if I said 'sorry'?" he asked, giving her another naughty grin.

She pouted up at him, enjoying the warmth of his hands covering her small fists. "You can try. But only after letting go of my hands."

He shook his head. "Not if you plan to punch me again."

"Don't tempt me!"

He threw back his head and laughed, letting go of her hands with obvious reluctance. "I'm sorry. Put it down to sheer jealousy towards all the men you have met before you came into my life." He spoke in a hoarse voice which lifted every single one of her body hair in goose bumps.

"Aren't you a flirt?!" She took a few steps back to put some distance between the two of them, glad to find her erratic breathing slowing down once she was out of his proximity. "I really need to go. Thanks for the coffee and conversation. I…"

"Dinner?" He did not care that he was interrupting her. He simply could not let go of her without knowing when he was going to see her next. "Tonight?"

"Let me call you."

"Give me your number and I'll call you," he insisted.

"Okay." She gave him her cell number.

"Let me drop you home."

"I don't think it's…"

"I insist. After all, I've taken so much of your time this morning." He took her hand in his, drawing her towards the doorway.

"Won't you get late to work?"

He shrugged. "The company will survive if I get a few minutes late."

She laughed, impressed with his confidence despite herself. He was not just handsome, but so smart too. And he surely must be intelligent if he was heading the finance department of Arjun Mathur's company, which was a mammoth enterprise. And Arjun was not one to suffer fools gladly.

"What do you do?" he asked, opening the door to his brilliant blue Audi which was parked in front of the bungalow.

"I run a modelling agency; from my home actually." She did not mention that it was one of the more successful ones in India, let alone Mumbai.

"Sounds interesting. How does it work?"

She was startled to notice that they were at the gates to her bungalow by the time she gave him a brief about her company. She had always lived in the bungalow which had belonged to the Sanyals for three generations. While Mudit had not been living all that far away from the time he was a preteen. It had taken him barely seven minutes to drive her over. Talk about a small world!

He got out of the car and was opening her door even before she had unclipped her seat belt, impressing her with his chivalry. Taking her hand in his, he helped her out of the car. "You didn't really have to do it, you know," she protested.

"I didn't have to, yes. But I needed to, as much as I need to breathe."

Dipika tumbled head long in love with the man who was studying her with his deep grey eyes as if he was etching her face into his memory for eternity. Only, she did not recognise the emotion for what it was. "Are you going to kiss me goodbye?" she asked, her voice hoarse with longing.

"Try and stop me." Letting go of her hand, he leaned forward to take her mouth greedily, not touching her otherwise. If he took her in his arms, he knew for a fact that he would have bundled her right back into his car and driven her back to his house.

They parted ways with obvious reluctance, Mudit finally driving the car out of the driveway as if the devil was on his tail.

3

"Who was that?" asked Krish, walking down the staircase even as Dipika entered the main hall of the bungalow.

"Who was who?" she answered her brother's question with one of her own as she stalled for time; willing the hot colour to recede from her face. A photographer by profession, Krish Sanyal was too observant and right now she was so damn shell-shocked and nowhere near ready to share anything about the weird emotions she was feeling for a near stranger; reeling under them actually.

"The person who was driving out of our compound like a fire engine called for duty." Krish studied his sister's blushing face minutely, curious about who had dropped her home. "I thought you went for a jog?"

"Yes, I did."

"But someone obviously drove you home. Is everything alright?" He moved forward to take her elbow in his hand and drew her towards the kitchen. "I need coffee. How about you?"

"Maybe later. I had some just now."

"Aah! It was a coffee date." Krish lifted a thick eyebrow in query as he filled a large mug with the brew their cook Narasimha had poured into a tall, insulated stainless steel urn which managed to keep it hot through the day, before adding some milk and sugar.

Dipika rolled her eyes, refusing to respond to her brother's teasing words. Away from Mudit's stimulating presence, she had begun to feel low. To begin with, she was astounded at herself. She still could not believe that she had let him kiss her the way he had. Not just that, but the way she had responded to him, with an equal enthusiasm. Maybe even a tad more fervent than he had been. It was so unlike her. Well, she was not exactly a shy person; but still managed to keep people at arms' length, especially those belonging to the opposite sex.

Okay, she was not a virgin, having had a brief affair when she was barely twenty. Right now, she could not even recall Vijay's features clearly. They had been to college together and all she had to say about their affair was that they had both been scratching an itch. The fling had been brief, and had fizzled out as neither had felt an interest to prolong it. At best, it had been a mediocre experience.

As for Mudit's kiss at the beach… Dipika shook her head to herself. Her whole body trembled with a strange urge whenever she thought about it. And she seemed to be thinking about it all the time. And again, there was the kiss in his library. Deeper, more sizzling, more mind-numbing. But why?

And just now, after getting out of his car, she had actually challenged Mudit if he was going to kiss her. And of course, he had risen to the challenge beautifully before kissing her senseless.

What was different about Mudit? And what had happened to her idea of keeping men at arms' length? It was as if a tornado had entered her life and swept her off her feet.

"Dip?" Krish turned his surprised gaze to his sister's slouched shoulders as she stood next to the coffee counter, staring unseeingly at a tray full of mugs. Placing a hand on her shoulder, he turned her towards himself, asking, "What's the matter?"

Dipika lifted her troubled gaze to look up at Krish, shaking her head from side to side. Crossing her arms below her chest, she sniffed loudly before saying, "I don't really know."

"Are you in love?" asked her brother bluntly.

"Eh? Are you mad?" She glared at him, her brown eyes spitting fire. The discovery that she had some strong feelings towards Mudit was still too new, too raw, to be shared with anyone else, even if it was her own sibling, whom she was close to. And she did not think it was love anyway. How was it possible to fall in love with a stranger?

Krish's eyes, exactly the same shade as hers, danced mischievously. "Methinks the boot's on the other foot," he said softly, giving her a broad wink.

"Bastard!" She rained her fists on his broad chest, unable to stop herself from laughing too. She shared a wonderful rapport with her brother and could never stay angry with him for long.

He threw his right arm around her shoulders, hugging her close to his side. "Why don't you get yourself a cup of coffee and let's talk all about it."

She shifted out of his hold to give him a wary glance. "About what?"

"Mmm." He took a sip of his coffee and savoured it even as he studied her troubled face. "About the person who dropped you home just now. What else? Would you like me to shoot the man for you?"

"You have gone mad!" She declared, turning around to fill a mug with steaming coffee and mixing in some milk and sugar. "I can't believe I've aroused your killer instincts."

"Hahaha! There is shooting and then some. I was talking about shooting with my camera, sister dear. What did you understand?"

Dipika gave Krish another mock glare, shaking her head at him before walking towards the garden room at one corner of the house. "Very funny," she muttered as he fell into step with her.

Krish sat down on a window sill and waited for Dipika to settle down on the adjacent sill before lifting an eyebrow at her. "Why don't you spill it all out?"

"Mudit Trivedi is his name," said Dipika, never having been able to keep a secret from her older brother, not since the time she was a baby. The only time she had held back anything from him was when Sanjana had given birth to Kabir and Dipika had recognised the baby as belonging to Krish. At that time, she had been unable to deny Sanjana's plea as to keeping the baby's father's name a secret.

"I know Mudit. I met him through Arjun. Go on!" Krish smiled encouragingly at his sister.

Dipika sighed. "So he said."

"How did you meet him? Have you known him long?" Krish wanted to know everything at once.

"Last night at the *dandiya*. Surprisingly, I met him again today while jogging on Versova beach. I've been jogging every day, like forever. But have never come across him before today," declared Dipika in a surprised voice.

"Don't you usually go jogging before six?" asked Krish, keeping his empty coffee mug down to focus completely on his sister.

"That's true. But I woke up late today. I…"

"Maybe Mudit went jogging at his usual time. And it was you who went later than usual…"

Dipika snapped her fingers, amazed at the way things had turned out. "You could be right."

"I know I'm right," said Krish, his handsome face smug as he grinned at her.

"Meh!" responded Dipika, silently agreeing with him. After all, had Mudit not mentioned that he went jogging every morning along the beach?

"So, what happened?" Krish was curious to know more.

She shrugged. "Not much, really." She looked down at her finger nails, unable to meet her brother's sharp gaze. "I went to his house for a short while, which is where I had coffee. I…"

"You went home with a total stranger?" Krish wiggled his eyebrows, teasing her mercilessly.

"Krish Sanyal, enough!" Dipika shouted suddenly, glaring at her sibling. "I'm not going to tell you anything more."

"Hey! Are you guys quarrelling?" Sanjana stepped into the garden room with a brimming coffee mug, her eyes searching both their faces. While her husband was grinning from ear to ear, her sister-in-law had a disturbed expression on her lovely face.

"Me quarrelling? Never!" declared Krish, reaching across to pull his wife into his arms and giving her a brief, but torrid kiss. "Good morning, sweetheart! Sleep well?" he asked in a soft and adoring voice.

"Mmm." Sanjana melted in his arms for but a few seconds before slipping out to look at Dipika. "Dip? Are you alright? Tell me if you want me to kick your brother for you," she offered. It went to show the depth of their friendship that Sanjana was ready to kick the husband she loved from the bottom of her heart. But then, Krish tended to tease people mercilessly, especially his little sister.

Dipika giggled, smiling at her best friend. "Thanks, Sanju, but no. I wouldn't want to miss that particular pleasure." She turned around to thumb her nose at Krish.

He lifted his hands in front of his chest in a defensive gesture. "I think you girls are ganging up against me," he grumbled. "Time to bring in some reinforcements. Is Kabir awake?"

"Not yet. And don't you dare wake him up," said his wife, in mock threat. She had allowed her son to sleep in as he had stayed awake until way past two am.

"As if!" Krish's gaze promised retribution as he gave his wife a long look. "I'm off to get more coffee," he said, going towards the kitchen.

"What's up?" asked Sanjana.

Dipika gave a long sigh. "Mudit happened."

"Someone I know?"

"You probably do. He says he's Krish's friend."

"Are you talking about Mudit Trivedi? The guy who works with Arjun Mathur?" asked Sanjana, her eyes lighting up playfully.

"The very same. And what's so funny about that?" asked Dipika, glaring at her sister-in-law.

"Not funny funny. But I think he's damn hot and a gentleman at that. If Krish doesn't have all my love, I might have considered setting my cap at Mudit," she declared, tongue firmly tucked in cheek.

"Oh really!" Dipika arched her eyebrows at Sanjana.

Sanjana nodded. "Arjun's wife Kiara and Mudit are great friends. She swears by him."

Dipika had met Kiara a couple of times, but did not know her all that well.

"Mudit happened on you when? You met him at the dance yesterday?" Sanjana was dying to know more.

"Surprisingly, I not only met him for the first time at the dance last night; but again, today morning when I went jogging…"

"Twice in less than twenty-four hours! Now that's definitely not a coincidence. Or is it?"

Dipika gave her friend a weak grin. "It is. That was what…"

"…I was telling her," interrupted Krish, walking back into the garden room. "Dip goes jogging every day at around six am. So does Mudit, but later in the morning. But today, she got delayed because of the late night from the *dandiya* and happened to meet Mudit at the beach. And the rest, as they say, is history.

Dipika placed her fisted hands on her slender hips, tilting her head back to glower up at her brother. "What history?" she growled.

"You going home with him."

"You went to Mudit's home?" Sanjana's voice was a delighted squeal. "You didn't mention that to me."

"As if I had a chance," grumbled Dipika, continuing to glare at her brother.

Krish laughed loudly. "Come on, Sis. Why are you angry with me? I think you both will make a great match."

"Match? You've gone mad, Krish." Dipika could not believe her ears. In all these years, Krish had never tried to push her into the arms of any man. What was happening now? Was he doing it because he was a happily married man these days?

Sanjana placed a restraining hand on her husband's forearm, giving him a warning glance from the corner of her eyes. Krish was being a tad over enthusiastic, which was something even she found surprising.

"Okay, okay! There's no need for you both to team up against me. I like Mudit. He's not just decent, but extremely smart too. That's why…"

Dipika would not let him finish his sentence. She slammed a fist into his shoulder, hurting herself more than she did her brother, giving him a sarcastic smile as she said, "So are a number of guys I know. Buzz off, bro!"

"Do you think the lady is protesting too much?" asked Krish, rolling his eyes at the ceiling before throwing an arm around Dipika's shoulders. "Did I also mention that he's working for Arjun's company as the youngest financial director? Chill, Dip. It was just a thought, okay? There's no need for you to bash me up."

Dipika leaned her head against his shoulder, confused by the strong emotions roiling through her. Generally calm, she was surprised by the way she had lost her temper at Krish's teasing. But then, meeting Mudit had rattled her more than she cared to admit. As for the other information her brother mentioned, she was not at all surprised that he held a high post in Arjun Mathur's company.

And his kisses... she sighed softly. She still could not understand how he had got away with them! And so early in the morning too. She felt a smile tug at one corner of her mouth when she thought of the man's confidence; and the way he had taken her hand and walked over to his house without even a by-your-leave.

She liked him! Yes!

Mudit was thoroughly distracted as he sat in front of his laptop, his mind swirling around the beautiful Dipika. It was Saturday morning and not everyone worked at Mathur Industries. But both Arjun and Mudit put in a few hours of work on most Saturdays. Though recently it had been only Mudit who had been a regular as Arjun preferred to spend his Saturdays with his wife.

Today, Mudit had been unable to concentrate on his work and had been wondering if he should simply give up and call it a day. Which was a first for him in the eight years he had been working with Mathur Industries. And it was not as if he had never had a girlfriend before now. But no woman had ever come between him and his work.

Does it mean Dipika is my girlfriend? A goofy grin split up his face at the thought as he stared at the finance report of the last quarter.

"Hey, are you busy?" Arjun pushed open the door to Mudit's cabin and peeped in. "What's funny?" he asked, noticing the wide grin on his friend's face.

"To answer your first question, I'm not." Mudit grimaced. "In fact, I'm unable to concentrate and have been wondering if I should simply shut shop for the day."

"And that's funny?" Arjun stepped inside to sit on the corner of his financial director's desk.

"Actually, no," muttered Mudit, staring down at his keyboard.

"What's the matter?" Arjun was surprised to see that his friend was refusing to meet his gaze. It had never happened before today.

Mudit finally looked up. "Forget it, Arjun. You wanted something?"

"Do you wanna take off for an early lunch?" asked Arjun. "All expenses paid," he added, giving Mudit a wink.

"Will you throw in a couple of beers?" asked Mudit, lifting an eyebrow at his boss, closing his laptop before getting up from his chair.

Arjun nodded. "If you want."

"Where's Kiara?" asked Mudit, suddenly realising that Arjun wanted to have lunch with him on a Saturday, instead of spending time with his darling wife whom he was crazy about.

"Travelling on work," grimaced Arjun, missing his wife badly. She had only left the previous day and was planning to return by Monday evening. Kiara was a professional hacker, which was how she had met Arjun Mathur; when he needed to find out how funds were being embezzled from his company. Kiara's parents lived in the bungalow next to Mudit's and the two of them had known each other from the time they were children. It was Mudit who had introduced Kiara to Arjun.

"During the weekend?" he asked now, giving Arjun a sympathetic glance.

"Yes, during the weekend," grumbled Arjun.

"You should have gone with her."

"She didn't want me underfoot," growled Arjun. And he could not really blame her. Her job was intense and required a lot of concentration. And this particular client had called her over to Delhi during the weekend as he didn't want his employees to know that he was hiring a hacker to find out how his ideas were being released by his competitor before he could do it himself. But that did not stop Arjun from missing her terribly. "But tell me what you were grinning about when I entered your office." Arjun was anything if not persistent.

Mudit sighed. "Nothing *yaar*. I met this woman last evening, then again today morning when I went jogging. Dipika Sanyal! She…"

"Are you talking about Krish's sister?" asked Arjun, giving Mudit a surprised glance as they stepped outside the entrance to the office building. Arjun's driver brought his car to a halt at the front right at that moment.

"You know her, of course."

"Of course." Arjun gave Mudit a teasing glance. "I think you must be smitten if you have started grinning at your laptop." He laughed outright when Mudit groaned.

Shutting the car door after settling down next to Arjun, Mudit said, "You might be right. Only I didn't realise how bad it was until I couldn't focus on the quarterly report."

"Aah! Now that says it all." Arjun turned to his driver to instruct him. "Drive over to The Hilton near the T2 airport."

"Yes, sir," responded the driver as he turned the car towards the gates.

"Doesn't it?" grimaced Mudit, continuing his conversation with his friend. "I have invited her for dinner tonight. But she hasn't said 'yes' yet." Which was another thing which was bothering him. He had been sure that Dipika wanted to get to know him too. After all, she had responded so well to his kisses, giving as much as she got, hadn't she?

"Now what are you grinning about?" Arjun gave the other man a curious glance, not missing the ruddy colour on Mudit's clean shaven cheeks. "Don't tell me you're blushing?" he teased.

"Hahaha!" Mudit refused to respond as he continued to grin to himself, thinking of the time he had spent with Dipika that morning. He willed strongly that she agreed to go to dinner with him in the evening.

Mudit seems to have met his match in your sister I believe!

Arjun quickly typed into his phone before sending the message to his friend Krish, adding a winky face emoji at the end.

Hahaha! I said the same words to Dip and got slammed for my efforts. Though she's definitely smitten.

Krish responded almost instantaneously, adding a high-five emoticon to his message.

So is he! This is going to be fun to watch, hehe!

Arjun also pinged his wife regarding the matter, enjoying himself immensely. He was truly glad for Mudit's sake though. What his friend needed was someone to love him. Mudit had been heartbroken when his grandfather died three years ago. He had considered Shiamak Trivedi his only family, even though he had a pair of parents and three siblings, all living in Surat. He did not care for his estranged family members, not one of them; not after he came to live with his grandfather right here in Mumbai at the tender age of twelve.

Arjun came out of his reverie when his car entered the portals of The Hilton. He watched Mudit with a lot of amusement when the latter had only half a beer and managed to eat small bites of the starters before refusing to order anything from the main course.

Yes, Mudit had caught it hard indeed!

4

It was past two when Mudit took a cab from the hotel as he and Arjun had to go in different directions. He eagerly removed his cell phone from his jeans pocket when it rang, confident that it must be Dipika who was calling him.

He scowled in disappointment when he saw Tanvi's picture on the screen, wondering if he should avoid the call. But no! If he did that, chances were high that she would call him again.

"Hi!" greeted Mudit briefly after taking the call.

"Heya Mudit! I thought we should meet for dinner tonight. We can even avoid going to the *dandiya* if you don't want to." After thinking long and hard; and also talking to a couple of her best friends, Tanvi had arrived at the erroneous conclusion that Mudit probably did not want to go dancing. That was why she had decided to sacrifice the dance this Saturday evening, all for the man she planned to marry soon.

"Er…" Mudit quickly thought on his feet. Even if Dipika did not agree to go out with him, he was sure he was not keen to spend the evening with Tanvi. He had noticed that his interest in her had been steadily waning over the last few weeks. Meeting Dipika had helped him make up his mind. "I'm kind of busy this evening, Tanvi. I…"

"Busy?" Tanvi's voice was a screech in his ear. "But why? Hadn't we planned to go to the *dandiya* on all the nine nights of Navratri?" Her voice wobbled as she swayed between losing her temper and crying aloud.

As for Mudit, he recalled her mentioning about the *dandiya* nights some weeks ago. And he had even attended some of those until last evening. But he had not really taken her seriously, not about going on all nine nights. After all, she must be aware that it was not in his nature to go dancing every night of the festival. If she did not understand even that much about him after dating him for six months, then it was simply too bad. "That had probably been your plan," he muttered. "But I find it rather suffocating."

"Suffocating? How dumb is that? It's happening in a large, open-air ground. How can one suffocate there?" Tanvi took his words literally and shouted at him. She wanted to throw something at his stubborn head. Grr! Why was he doing this to her now? Mudit had seemed to be such a wonderful partner, always polite and well behaved. He had been so chivalrous and attentive too. But then, she was not to know that the Gemini had two faces, entirely different from one another. During the six months they had been seeing each other, Tanvi had got to experience the polite and nice side of Mudit. It was only now when he had decided he was not interested in her any longer, that his rude side had surfaced. Tanvi was flummoxed at the unexpected change in the man she had been training to become her husband in the not-too-far future. He appeared like a different person altogether.

That set her thinking about the time they had spent together. It was six months since they began dating on and off. Mudit had somehow managed to remain elusive, refusing to commit himself to her beyond a few kisses. Not for want of trying on her part, definitely not. But the man was as slippery as an eel. While all her friends had met him and believed Mudit was her boyfriend, she did not know any of his. In which case, did anyone he knew think she was his girlfriend at all? While she had introduced him to her brother and sister, she had not met any member of his family. She did not even know if he had one. Damn!

Phew! Mudit thrust his lower lip out to let some steam off. Was she really so dumb? How had he even imagined that he was attracted to such a woman? "Listen, Tanvi, I…"

"You listen, Mudit. I think you are not being very nice to me." Her voice wobbled as she uttered the words. Taking a deep breath to calm down, she continued, "You promised to go with me to the *dandiya* on all evenings. And here I am, sacrificing one whole evening for your sake; and you can't even appreciate it."

Mudit rolled his eyes towards the ceiling of the cab, not saying anything in response to her words. What was the use? It did not seem as if she was in a state of mind to listen to him. "You are right. I am unable to appreciate this 'sacrifice' as you call it. Did you ever bother to find out what I might want to do? How I would like to spend my evenings?

It is always about what Tanvi wants. You want to go to the movies, *dandiya*, high end restaurants, discos, et al. It is always about you. What about me? I may…" He stopped when he heard a howling sound. Taking the instrument off his ear, he stared at it dumbfounded. Was she crying? Or snarling maybe? Hearing a roaring noise, he moved the phone back to his ear to find out what the hell was happening.

"How dare you?" she wailed. "How dare you say that? I ask you every time before getting the tickets booked. You…"

He tuned off, completely disgusted. She informed him, usually. And it was he who booked the tickets, every time. After all, he was the man. He was expected to bear all the costs of dating. That much Tanvi was clear about.

"Mudit!" Tanvi was screaming by now. "Do you hear me, you idiot?"

"I'm sure more than half of Mumbai can hear you," grumbled Mudit, disgusted by the way she was trying to control him. How the hell had he put up with it for this long?

"You have no respect for me," she shouted.

"You are right, I don't. Shall we get off the phone now?" he asked, his voice cold enough to freeze the Arabian Sea.

"You will hang up on me?" she asked, so startled that she stopped crying.

"I am asking you to do the honours." The biting sarcasm was lost on her.

"Eh?"

"You cut the call, damn it," he snarled. Otherwise, she would only keep on hounding him. He knew it for sure.

"I hate you, you bastard!"

Mudit let out a huge sigh of relief when she finally disconnected the phone. Phew! That had been some scene. He mopped his sweating face with a handkerchief, tucking his phone back into his jeans pocket. This was not the right time to speak to Dipika. He needed to really cool down before he did that. How he wished he had had more beer during lunch. Only, he had not wanted to be sloshed, not before his grand dinner date.

Which he was not so sure was going to happen. His mouth drooping at the corners, Mudit got out of the cab to go inside his house, thoroughly annoyed. He could not believe that it was only that morning when Dipika had spent some time with him at his house. It all seemed such a long time ago.

Ping!

That was his phone. Only Mudit was not sure he wanted to see any message. Most probably it was from Tanvi and he was up to his neck with his ex-girlfriend. Deciding to delete the message without reading it, he opened his phone to be pleasantly surprised. It was from Dipika.

Hey, dinner this evening works for me. Where should I meet you?

With a wide smile on his face, he quickly typed his response.

I'll pick you up, babe. 7 pm?

Perfect! I'll be ready. Looking forward.

Hahaha! Mudit laughed out long and loud, forgetting all about the earlier scene with Tanvi. He was too damn thrilled that Dipika had agreed to go out for dinner with him.

Yes!

5

"You didn't tell me we were going to ride on a bike." Dipika stared at the black monster, aghast. She was wearing a short red dress with a narrow skirt and was not sure how she would be able to sit pillion. Otherwise, she would have been thrilled to ride the BMW which appeared all sleek and shiny.

Mudit, who had been admiring her long legs clad in black calf-length leather boots with four-inch stiletto heels, lifted his gaze up to meet hers, a grimace forming on his face. "Sorry about that. But I left my car at work. So!" He shrugged. "I can help you settle on the bike," he offered, a lopsided grin stretching his mouth to the left.

Dipika could not stop the answering smile from lighting up her face. "Tell you what? I know my car isn't an Audi. But can we take it instead of your bike?" She drove a red Volkswagen Virtus which was less than four months old.

"Lead the way," he said, taking her elbow in his. "But wait. I need a kiss before that."

Before he could gather her in his arms, Dipika placed her palms on his chest, her pulse spiking when she felt the hardness of firm flesh tightly stretched over powerful muscles. "No, Mudit."

"But why not?" he asked, looking deeply into her shimmering brown gaze. "It has been so long."

"You are crazy, aren't you? We only met this morning and you've already stolen a kiss from me." Actually, way more than one kiss. While she held his gaze steadily, all she wanted to do was to sink into his delicious body and forget all about dinner. Which is exactly why she did not want him to kiss her. She barely knew the man and was not at all keen on jumping into bed with him. It was only too obvious that that was exactly what his intention was.

"Tell me you didn't enjoy our kisses and I won't ask again." He ran his large hands up and down over her bare arms, smiling when he felt the goose bumps coming to life on her skin. Nor did he miss the colour riding high on her slim cheeks. Her luscious lips appeared too damn inviting, a gorgeous shade of red, shining under the fairy lights strung on the many trees and shrubs in the Sanyals' garden.

She turned her face to the side, not at all keen for him to read the longing in her eyes. "You know I did." A typical Libra, she was inherently truthful and not one to hide behind lies.

"Then what's stopping you?" He leaned over to press his lips to the pulse beating at the side of her neck, right below her ear. Unable to resist, he stroked the area with the tip of his tongue, smiling when he heard her moan.

"Mudit…"

"Hmm…"

"Shall we go? I don't want Krish to find us here."

That brought him back to his senses pretty fast. He did not want her brother to murder him, not before their first date. "You sure know how to cool a man's ardour, don't you?" he grumbled, taking a couple of steps back. Though his gaze continued to scorch her.

"Hehe! Do you good." She led him to her car which was parked at the back of the bungalow.

He gave a soft whistle when he saw the red Virtus. "Cool!"

"Do you want to drive?" she asked, removing the key from her black clutch purse, and offering it to him.

"Only if you don't mind."

She shook her head. "I don't."

"Let's go then." He opened the passenger door and waited for her to settle in before walking around the bonnet to get into the driver's seat. He adjusted the seat to fit his long frame comfortably before turning the rear-view mirror to suit himself. "This is an amazing car."

"Glad you like it. I gifted it to myself on my birthday." And she was damn proud of it.

"And when is your birthday?" he asked, turning the car around the compound towards the gate.

"September 28. When is yours?"

"28? What a coincidence! Mine is on May 28. Let me see, that makes you a Libra, right?"

"Hmm. And you are a Gemini. Twin-faced. One needs to be careful while dealing with a Gemini guy."

"How so?" He gave her a corner-eyed glance before taking a left turn. "Are you saying that it's not as difficult dealing with a Gemini girl?" he asked, tongue firmly tucked in his cheek.

Dipika laughed. "You know what I mean."

He grimaced. "I do. Even I'm surprised by the way my thoughts and opinions swing like a pendulum. At times, they drive me nuts."

"Aww, you poor baby." She gave him a devilish grin.

"You look lovely," he said, confounding her with the sudden change in topic.

Dipika took a deep breath to calm down her catapulting blood pressure. Finding that it was not enough, she took a few more breaths before responding to him. It was not as if she had never received compliments from the male of the species. The opposite was true, in fact. But coming from Mudit who appeared so damn hot himself, it was enough to set her nerves sizzling. "Thank you. You don't look so bad yourself," she finally responded, turning to give him a long glance.

He was wearing a pair of dark blue jeans teamed with an open-necked white shirt and a linen jacket in the colour of rich cream. He appeared wider in the smart casual attire, than in the t-shirt he had been wearing that morning. And Dipika couldn't help but admire a smartly turned-out man. His short and thick, dark hair was brushed back neatly while his finger nails were clean and neatly filed. And she had not missed his long feet clad in dark brown leather loafers. Their sight made her curious to know how he would appear in his bare feet.

Ruddy colour rose up Mudit's cheeks when he heard her compliment. Taking his left hand off the steering wheel, he took her right hand and lifted it to his mouth, kissing the back. "Thanks."

"Mudit…" Her heart thumped in longing even as she gently tried to prise her hand from his. "Please…"

"Please what? Are you aware that you are distracting me, Dippy?" He let go of her hand to focus on his driving.

Not as much as he was distracting her. But then, she was not at the wheel, which was a good thing. She was not sure if she could have managed it, not with the live-wire seated next to her. His very presence teemed with such electricity that she felt she might get short-circuited at any moment. "Where are we going?" she asked.

"Yauatcha is a Cantonese restaurant in Bandra Kurla Complex. I've booked a private dining room there. Have you been there before?"

Dipika shook her head. "Nope. I've heard a lot about it though."

"Do you like Oriental food?" he asked, turning to give her yet another glance before returning his focus to the road.

"Love it. How about you? Are you vegetarian?"

"Yes, to both." He brought the car to a halt in front of the restaurant. Getting out, he handed the car key over to a valet before walking around to open the passenger door.

"Would you mind if I order non-veg dishes?" she asked as he helped her out of the car. It was not that she did not like vegetarian food. But she wanted to know if he would object if she wanted to eat chicken or fish at the same table he was dining at.

"Of course not, babe. It's your evening. You can have anything you want." He leaned down to whisper into her ear. "Even yours truly for dessert."

Dipika shivered when she heard his words. But it was the soft brush of his lips against her ear which made her body go up in flame. The man was a charmer, definitely. And she so wanted to keep him at arms' length, at least until she got to know him better. It was not enough that he was Krish's friend.

She shook her head at him. "Flirt!"

"Guilty!" he said, taking her hand in his before walking into the delightful ambience of Yauatcha and giving his name to the woman who appeared to be in charge. "I've booked a private dining room for 8 pm."

"That's right, Mr. Trivedi. This way, please." She guided them to the left side and pushed open a heavy door which led into a large room which could comfortably seat ten people. Except that there was only one table arranged for two set right in the middle of the room; the myriad perfumes of brightly lit candles and colourful flowers arranged in exotic bouquets greeting them.

"This is lovely, thanks," said Mudit, giving the woman a charming smile.

Rogue! That's what he is, thought Dipika, noticing the colour rushing up the woman's face as she smiled in acknowledgement of his words. *A rogue with faultless manners.*

He pulled a chair out for Dipika and waited for her to sit down before going to settle down in the chair opposite. Handing her the cocktail menu, he opened a second one to check out what was on offer.

"This is a beautiful place," said Dipika, her gaze on her date, rather than on the menu.

"I'm glad you like it," he said. "What would you like to drink?" he asked.

"What do you recommend?"

He shrugged. "I don't really know. This is my first visit too." He gave her an irresistible grin.

She smiled brightly on hearing his words, happy that he had not brought any other woman to this restaurant. "Let's see what they have to offer."

Soon, they were sipping on fruity cocktails and munching into dumplings—chicken and coriander dim sums for Dipika and ones with asparagus and water chestnuts for Mudit. The conversation flowed comfortably until Dipika suddenly recalled the woman who had been clinging to his arm at the *dandiya*. She went quiet, not really knowing how to ask him about it.

"Come on, spit it out. What's bothering you?" he asked, taking her left hand in his right one.

"Nothing."

He shook his head. "I refuse to accept that." She had been all chirpy and chatty barely a moment ago.

A deep sigh shuddered through Dipika. She was not at all keen on rocking the boat as they had been having such a good time until she recalled the woman at the *dandiya*. But then, her mind was working furiously and she could not simply forget her. She had been so beautiful too. Dipika hoped against hope that Mudit was not two-timing her. But then, he owed her no loyalty as he was not really her boyfriend. They were just two people having dinner together.

"Dippy?" Mudit pressed his thumb into the centre of her palm, looking deeply into her eyes, as if willing her to tell him the truth.

"That evening at the *dandiya*…"

"Yes, what about it?" he asked, stroking her palm with his thumb now, ever so gently.

Dipika's eyes glazed over even as her blood began to sizzle. How could he do that by just touching her palm? Drawing a deep breath to bring her wandering thoughts together, she said, "There was this woman who…" She was not sure how to continue from there. She could not really tell him that the said woman had been clinging to his arm, could she?

"Aah! You noticed." He gave her a wide and satisfied smile, like that of a cat which had had its fill of a bowl full of cream.

Dipika removed her hand from his hold to sit up straight. She sipped from her cocktail, more because she was not keen for him to notice her trembling lips. So! He was not even going to hide his connection to another woman. A man about town, it seemed. It looked like this was going to be their first and last date.

He watched her minutely, amused to notice her smile disappearing completely. That was when it struck him that he had never seen her face without a smile. He also realised that he would do anything to bring the smile back to her lovely face. "That was Tanvi Desai. I used to date her."

"Oh!" She sipped from her glass once again, studying his face carefully. If he 'used' to date her, what had she been doing clinging to his arm last evening? "Until when?" she asked.

"Why do you want to know?" he asked, curiosity lighting up his grey eyes. He knew she was attracted to him. But he wanted to hear her admit to it in so many words.

"Eh? I don't go out with a man who is in a relationship with another woman." Dipika glared at him. She was startled to feel the pain in the region of her chest when she thought that she might not be able to set eyes on Mudit ever again.

"What kind of a cad do you think I am?" he asked, his own smile disappearing as a serious expression settled over his face.

A flush darkened Dipika's features as she gave him a regretful glance. "I don't think you are a cad, Mudit. But then, I'm going by what I saw last night. You can't deny that the woman was clinging to you." There! She had said it aloud, about what was bothering her.

"Did you feel jealous?" he asked, the smile back on his face, stretching his sexy mouth wide, catching her avid gaze.

Dipika shook her head slowly; stopped before giving a small nod. "Yes, I did."

"Oh babe!" He pushed his chair back to get up and take the few steps which brought him right next to her chair. Pulling her out of her seat, he gathered her against his massive chest. Placing a hand at the back of her neck, he lifted her face up to his before brushing his mouth over hers.

Dipika moaned, throwing her arms around his neck to draw him closer as she opened her mouth to his invasion, sighing when she felt him exploring her mouth eagerly with a thorough sweep of his tongue. While she did not know all that much about Mudit, one thing she could say about the man: he was a fabulous kisser. By the time he was finished checking out the contours of her mouth, she was feeling totally breathless and was clinging to him like a limpet. Or she might simply have melted into a puddle on the floor at his feet. Such was the effect of his heated kiss.

"Mudit…" She turned her face to lean it on his shoulder, breathing heavily, sliding her arms around his lean waist.

"Dippy…" he responded; his chin pressed to the top of her head as he tried to control his raging libido. He had had a few affairs in his time and even kissed Tanvi many times during the last six months; but nothing had aroused him to a fever pitch, the way kissing the woman in his arms did. It was an effort not to take her right here on the floor of the private dining room. And it looked like he would not give a damn even if a waiter walked in on them. Such was his fervour. He ran his hand down her trembling back, trying to bring a sense of calmness, without really succeeding. One thing pleased him though; she was as aroused as he was, if not more. A smile lit his face before stretching into a full-blown grin.

With a soft sigh, Dipika lifted her face from his shoulder to look up at him right at that moment. "What's funny?" she asked, noticing the grin on his face.

He shook his head slowly from side to side. "I'm just amazed at how much I desire you, a woman I barely know. Believe me, it has never happened to me before now."

"And that's funny?" she asked, smiling despite herself when she heard how much he desired her.

He laughed softly, leaning over to touch his forehead to hers. "Not funny, but it feels good, making me want to smile."

"Aah!" Her gaze clung to his, unable to look away from the heat she perceived in his grey eyes.

"I want to love you, Dippy, fully." He placed a hand over her mouth when she would have interrupted. "I don't mean immediately, but whenever you are ready. Just thought I should keep you warned."

He was being completely honest with her and she truly appreciated that. Pulling his face down to hers—he was an inch taller than her despite the four-inch heels she was wearing—she kissed him on his mouth, taking a gentle bite of his thick lower lip.

Mudit groaned loudly as the gesture sent blood shooting to his lower body, making his shaft grow hard with longing. But he waited patiently, wondering what she was going to do next.

Dipika drew the tip of her tongue over the shape of his lips before pressing it in the middle, seeking entry.

He opened his mouth to let her in, groaning longer and louder this time.

She swiped her tongue leisurely through his mouth, enjoying the taste of vodka and all male before drawing his tongue into her mouth and sucking on it gently. She hastily threw her arms around his neck when she found herself a few inches above the floor as he lifted her in his arms and held her closer than ever, his rigid shaft throbbing against her abdomen.

But she refused to be distracted as she continued to kiss him, her heart rocking against her rib-cage as if it wanted to escape its confinement. Finally, unable to breathe, she let go of his tongue and lips to bury her face in the crook of his shoulder.

"I want you, babe." His voice was a growl against her ear as he bit her lobe before stroking it with the tip of his tongue.

Her breasts felt heavy and crushed against his hard chest, the nipples stiff and aching needily. She turned her head to accommodate his caresses, tremors running through her body when she felt the stroke of his damp tongue within the whorls of her ear. She gasped when she felt his large hands cupping her sensitised breasts, squeezing them gently. "Mudit..."

He turned her around in his arms before crushing her breasts in his hands, rubbing his palms over the stiffened nipples even as he nibbled along her jawline. "You taste so damn good."

Dipika was startled when he suddenly let go of her and pushed her into her chair. Even as she wondered what must have gone wrong, she heard him call out, "Come in." Hot colour bloomed on her cheeks when a waiter walked in, carrying their main course. She had been so lost in passion that she had not heard his knock. She stared at Mudit in a dazed manner and was unable to understand why he was standing at the window, looking outside.

"Leave it on the table, bro. We'll help ourselves." Mudit's voice was hoarse as he called out to the man while he continued to stand at the window facing the street, not at all keen for the guy to notice the state of his arousal.

"Yes sir." The waiter withdrew and shut the door behind him with a click.

Mudit turned around to walk to the dining table. "I'm sorry about that. Though I cannot take the full blame, Dippy. You make me forget myself."

"But you still heard the waiter knock on the door." She grimaced at herself as she pointed out.

"Haha! Aren't you glad that I did?" he asked, lifting an eyebrow at her as he studied the dishes on the table. Somehow, he had lost his appetite for food.

"Most definitely, yes," she muttered, staring at the food, finding the smell of it quite irritating.

"Let me serve you," he offered, lifting the serving spoon.

"No, Mudit. I'm not hungry," she said, a note of apology in her voice.

"Neither am I," he responded, letting the spoon fall back on the table with a clatter.

She shook her head slowly from side to side. "I think we both are a couple of idiots, wasting such wonderful food."

"Mmm. Tell you what! Let's pack the food and take it back to my house. What we both need is a dunk in my cold swimming pool. Don't you agree?" He gave her the lopsided smile once again, his eyes crinkling at the corners.

She laughed at that. "I think you're right. Though let me warn you. I can't swim to save my life."

"And I'm an Olympic level swimmer. I..."

"I don't know about swimming, but you sure have a bloated head, don't you?" she teased, laughing at him with her eyes.

"I'll let you know that I'm a swimming champion."

"Meh!" She poked her tongue at him.

"And I'll teach you."

"But I don't have a swim suit."

"Let's get one on our way home."

"Determined, aren't you?"

"As I mentioned, we need to cool down."

But in the end, the whole exercise turned out to be more arousing, what with the skin show Dipika put on in the bold, pink coloured bikini which he had insisted on buying her. As for Mudit, he looked good enough to eat in the briefest of blue shorts which hugged his manhood sexily, making her drool.

As for teaching her to swim, he was not so sure of being of much use as he could not think beyond kissing every exposed inch of her seductive body.

She sat on the lowest step at the shallow end of the pool, her hair swept up into a knot at the top of her head, her arms crossed over her chest. The water covered her up to her shoulders and she was glad of the small amount of privacy it gave her from the avid gaze of the man who had dived into the pool at the deep end.

Mudit swam slowly towards where she was sitting and trod water. "Want to learn to swim?"

"Maybe some other day," she said, her voice a croak as she gazed up at him, her eyes running greedily over his torso, the wide shoulders tapering down to a lean waist, forming a perfectly V-shaped body. Her heart was bouncing like a ping pong ball, up to her throat and then down to her stomach, making her breath shaky.

Abiding by her wish, he went to sit down on the step next to her, lifting the two glasses of red wine which he had poured earlier and handing one to her. "Cheers!" he said, touching the tip of his glass to hers.

"Cheers!" She leaned against his side with a soft sigh when he threw an arm around her waist to pull her close to his body.

"I thought we were here to cool down," he said, sipping from his wine as he studied the expressions chasing across her lovely face.

"So did I." She took a sip of wine before reaching over to place it on the tray at the side of the pool.

"It's not working, is it?" he asked conversationally, setting his wine glass aside to play with the strands of her hair which had broken loose from the top knot.

"Nope," she said, giving him a weak grin. "All this skin," she waved a hand while pointing at his chest, "is making me salivate."

"Tell me more." His voice was a growl of longing.

"Mudit! I think it's best if I went home."

"No."

"Then what do you want to do?" she asked, glaring up at him. Another few minutes, and she might throw herself into his arms and beg him to make love to her.

"Kiss every inch of your skin before burying myself deep inside you."

Her jaw dropped open as she stared up at him in amazement. "Then what's stopping you from doing exactly that?" she asked, her voice hoarse. Not giving him a chance to respond, she climbed into his lap before kissing him deeply. "I want you too, Mudit. Make love to me, now."

Lifting her in his arms, he got up from the step to climb outside the swimming pool before laying her down on a sun lounger. He lay beside her trembling body, throwing a leg over both of hers.

"*Mudit na Pappa.*" Sharda Trivedi carried a tray bearing a plate of *namkeen* and tea for her husband and went to sit next to him on the long wooden swing which had been in the family for more than one hundred years.

It was past seven in the evening and Chandulal Trivedi, Mudit's father, had only then returned home from work. He owned and ran a handicraft shop in Nanpura. It used to be a small rented shop at the time Mudit was a child. Unable to make two ends meet, Chandulal had jumped at the chance when his father, Shiamak Trivedi, who lived in Mumbai, offered to take care of Mudit. That was how Chandulal's eldest born had gone to live in Mumbai with his grandfather while the other three children, Arvind, Dinesh and Bhoomi, lived in Surat with their parents. These days, the shop was large with a two-thousand square feet area while the Trivedi family owned the premises.

"*Bolo,*" said Chandulal, sipping from the tea cup even as he ran his gaze over the multiple WhatsApp messages on his phone.

Sharda got pretty miffed. He was out the whole day, sometimes even on Mondays, which was a weekly holiday at the shop. After returning home this late, he still had no time for his wife. "Our neighbour, Nimesh Bhai, ran away with his best friend's wife today afternoon," she lied through her teeth, hoping to get a shocked reaction from her husband.

"Mmm. *Saaru*," said Chandulal, making his wife angrier than ever.

Sharda almost blew a fuse when she did not get the reaction she sought. It was obvious that Chandulal was not listening to her. She sniffed loudly, trying hard to catch his attention.

"*Shu thayu?*" he asked, lifting his gaze from the phone to look at his wife of thirty-four years. "*Tame kem gussa ma laago chho?*" He did not understand why she was angry with him.

"Did you hear what I said just now?" she asked, glowering at him.

"Of course, I did. You said… you said…" he paused, unable to recall her words, not even one of them. "Weren't you speaking about our children? That they have all gone out?" He took a wild guess as he could make out that none of the three youngsters seemed to be at home. They would have stepped out to greet him otherwise.

Sharda snorted, continuing to glare at him. "Just as I thought. You did not hear a word."

With a sigh, he placed the phone on the swing next to him and gave her his complete attention. "Alright, tell me now."

"I said that Nimesh Bhai ran away with his friend's wife," she said, her eyes dancing in a quick flash of amusement. She giggled when she saw the shocked expression on her husband's face.

"What? Are you sure about it? His poor wife. I..."

She burst out laughing, unable to stop as her mirth poured forth, her whole body shaking with it.

It was Chandulal's turn to glare at his wife. "What is wrong with you, *Mudit ni Mummy*? Our neighbour's house is on fire and you are laughing about it."

Sharda laughed long and hard before finally calming down. Shaking her head at her husband, she said, "I was fooling you. Rather, I was trying to shock you into speaking to me. But your reaction?" She laughed some more. "You said, 'mmm, *saaru*'." Giggles continued to shake her up.

"Very funny," he said, shaking his head at her. But a glimmer of a smile appeared on his face as he looked at his wife with affection. "So tell me. What did you want to actually tell me?"

"It's about Mudit. He is thirty-two years old and will be thirty-three in five months. Isn't it time to find him a wife?" she asked, looking at her husband eagerly. While she rarely got to meet her eldest born, she still felt a lot of affection for him.

Chandulal gave a long sigh, lifting a *chakli* from the snack plate and biting into it. He had no clue as to how to connect with his eldest son. When his father, Shiamak, had been alive, things had been easier. At least, Shiamak had acted as a bridge, keeping the family members in touch. But with him passing on, it was too difficult to communicate with Mudit. The boy was always polite and respectful. But that was all. He never spoke one word more than was absolutely necessary. Chandulal wondered if his son would even allow him to find him a marriage partner. And if he had a girlfriend, Mudit's family did not know anything about it.

"Have you spoken to him regarding this?" asked Chandulal.

"I thought we should both do the talking."

He sighed once again. "Do you want to call him after dinner?" he asked, his reluctance obvious.

Sharda nodded eagerly. "Yes, let us do that. It has been two weeks since I heard his voice."

Mudit, who had been tracing the curve of Dipika's jaw with his thumb, swore when his cell phone rang loudly from the lounger next to the one they were lying on.

Dipika laughed softly, a hand cupping his cheek. "Virulently colourful, aren't you?" she teased.

He breathed a sigh of relief when the phone stopped ringing only to swear some more when it began to ring again. "Excuse me, I might have to take this one." He reached across to take the phone and saw his father's face on the screen and felt as if a bucket of cold water had been upturned over his head. "Shit!" What bloody timing!

Dipika did not say anything as she sat up on the lounger before wrapping a towelling robe around her bikini-clad body. She gave a soft sigh, wondering if they were jumping into the physical part of their relationship a tad too soon.

Mudit got up to walk away from Dipika as he spoke into the phone. "*Ji* Pappa!"

"How are you, Mudit? Your mother and I have been missing you badly. Why don't you come home for a few days?" greeted his father in a guttural voice. The trouble was that there was no love lost between the two men; all because they had grown completely apart in the past two decades when Mudit had been living away from his immediate family.

"Let me try, Pappa, but I can't promise anything. With the year-end looming, I might not be able to get leave." Both of them knew he was lying, a white lie, but a lie nonetheless. Given a chance, Mudit would never bother to visit his family home in Surat. "How are you all doing?" he asked as an afterthought.

"We are all fine, son. You know your brothers Arvind and Dinesh have trained in diamond cutting and are now working with some big jewellers. They are earning very well too. As for your sister Bhoomi, she is in the last year of college. Your mother and I are thinking of getting her married soon after her graduation gets over."

"*Ji!*"

"But before that, Mudit. We want to see you settled." Sharda interjected as she had been following the conversation on the speaker. While the men were completely detached, she loved her son from the bottom of her heart and was truly upset by the estrangement. But somehow, she did not know how to reach out to him.

"Mamma! I hope you are doing well," greeted Mudit on hearing his mother's voice. He was not able to forgive her for letting go of him when he had been but a child.

"I'm fine, my son. What about you?"

"I'm doing great, Mamma. No issues."

"Don't you miss your family?" she asked in a pathetic voice.

He gave a bitter laugh. "I did, Mamma, when I was twelve years old. But I have grown up. Today, I am all of thirty-two and have no need for anyone."

Tears rolled down Sharda's face when she heard the bitterness in her son's voice. If only she could go back in time; maybe she would have stopped her husband from sending Mudit away. But then, that was asking for the impossible. "Forget all that. Let me tell you what we called you today about." She paused, waiting for some kind of response from him.

"Yes, Mamma." Mudit gritted his teeth, praying for patience. The cold January breeze had managed to freeze his libido which anyway had disappeared when he saw his father's face on the phone screen.

"There is this lovely girl, your father's best friend's daughter. Her name is Suchita. I think she will make you a perfect wife, Mudit. Why don't you make a plan to come home? You can meet her then."

Mudit rolled his eyes to the night sky. His parents were trying to arrange his marriage. And this was not the first time they had raised the subject with him. Only, now they had a suitable—according to them—girl's name as well. What kind of a joke was this? "I told you before, Mamma." He made an extra effort to keep his voice low so as to not hurt his mother. "I'm not interested in an arranged marriage."

"If it is love marriage you want, then are you in love with someone?" asked Chandulal, losing his patience.

"No, Pappa, I am not," said the son in a firm voice.

"In that case, what is your objection to meeting Suchita? As your mother mentioned, she is a sweet, *sanskari chhokri* who will make you an obedient wife."

Mudit took deep breaths to calm down his temper which was on the verge of blasting out of control. Who wanted an 'obedient' wife, damn it! "I need to go, Pappa. There is someone waiting for me."

"Before you go, what should I tell Suchita's parents?" asked Sharda, a desperate note in her voice.

"Why don't you ask them to find a nice, Gujarati *chhokra* and get their daughter married to him?" suggested Mudit. "*Aavjo*, Pappa, Mamma," he said, cutting the call before either of them could respond. While the Gujarati word meant 'see you soon', it was only a word as far as he was concerned as Mudit had no intention to see either of his parents, neither soon nor late.

He put his phone on silent before turning towards Dipika who was lying back on the lounger, wrapped in a towelling robe. He hoped that she was not going to tell him to go to hell. Walking swiftly over to where she was, he sat on the ground next to the lounger, crossing his legs. "Babe?"

Dipika's eyes were closed as she relaxed on the lounger. She was cosy once she had pulled on the robe around her bikini and she had decided to take a power nap while Mudit completed his call. Being a business woman herself, she did not find it strange that he was getting a call so late on a Saturday evening. And she simply was not the jealous sort. At least, she did not think so. Now she opened her eyes to look at the handsome Mudit who was sitting on the floor next to her. "Hey! That was some intense phone call."

"Tch! Yes," he responded briefly, his eyes studying her face searchingly. He was both hungry and angry by now and sex was the last thing on his mind. Talk about mood breaker!

"Listen Mudit." She sat up on the lounger, inadvertently drawing his gaze to her cleavage as the front of the robe fell open. Not that she was aware of it. "I hope you are hungry; because I am," she said.

He gave a sigh of relief, getting up immediately to take her hand in his and pull her to her feet. "I'm glad you asked. My stomach is growling actually," he said, giving her a small smile, which did not reach his eyes. He still could not let go of his anger towards his parents.

"Hey! Are you upset about something?" she asked, placing a hand in the middle of his chest. He had such a fabulous body that she did not seem to want to stop touching it. But she needed some nourishment first. And she was also keen to have a cheerful dinner partner.

He shrugged his massive shoulders, taking her hand in his to walk towards the back door of his bungalow. "The phone call. Let us eat first and talk later. And Dippy?" He stopped in his tracks to throw an arm around her shoulders. "I'm sorry about leaving you in the lurch like that," he whispered into her ear.

She turned her face to meet his gaze head on. "So am I. But it's for the best, I think. Or we would have jumped into bed without really knowing each other, right?"

"Mmm." He kissed her cheek before guiding her over to the dining room.

It was much later, way past midnight, when Mudit drove Dipika back to her house. Parking the car at the back, he waited until both were out of the car before pushing her against the side and leaned down to kiss her, a hand stroking the length of her bare left thigh.

She clung to him, her hands clutching his wide shoulders even as she greedily responded to his ardent kisses.

"You taste amazing," he growled, nibbling down the side of her jaw before burying his face in the crook of her neck. "I want you." Taking deep breaths to control his rising libido, he touched her racing pulse with the tip of his tongue.

As she leaned towards the side to accommodate his foraging mouth, Dipika took a deep breath before saying, "Mudit... I think it's best we wait for a while." The words themselves came out in gasps as she felt her blood pressure soar with each stroke of his tongue against the pulse beating at her neck.

"Wait for what?" he murmured, pulling her between his legs so that she could feel his hardened arousal.

Her hands running impatiently through his hair, she turned her head to take a sharp bite of his earlobe. "To make love."

He lifted his head to look down at her. "Until when?"

She shrugged, inadvertently drawing his gaze to her lush breasts as they jiggled with her movement. "Whenever."

"So why not today? Maybe even tomorrow?" He cupped her breasts in his hands, moving his palms over the nipples and smiling when they puckered in response.

Dipika sighed softly, revelling in his touch. "No."

He let go of her to turn away, running his hand through his hair. "Damn the phone call."

Dipika placed a hand on his taut forearm. "It was a good thing the call came, at the right time too. Let us take this a bit slow, Mudit. Please." She could understand his impatience as her own body craved his touch, his lovemaking, as desperately as a man seeking water in the middle of the desert.

He turned sideways to glance at her, the tautness leaving his body when he noticed her beautiful face and imploring eyes. "Okay, I'm not going to ask again, not until you beg me to love you."

She gave him a wide smile, pulling his face down for a kiss. "You're the best."

"If you say so," he growled before kissing her deeply. When they finally came up for air, he said, "I hope that keeps you awake the whole night."

She laughed softly, hugging him. "It's not what you did to me that is going to keep me awake. But what you didn't do to me."

"Serve you right."

She reached a hand and placed it over his fly, stroking down the length of his manhood, her eyebrow up in query as she gave him a teasing glance. "You going to sleep well tonight?"

Mudit groaned long and loud, wanting to protest, but liking her touch too much. "You're killing me, Dippy."

"Sorry." She removed her hand and placed it on his shoulder. "I think it's best you leave now."

"In a moment," he growled, pressing his cheek to hers even as he took deep breaths to calm down his clamouring body.

The next couple of weeks flew by as Mudit and Dipika met almost every day despite their busy schedules. They adjusted their timings for the morning jog, she delaying hers by half an hour and he bringing his own forward by the same amount of time. They left their phones behind as they concentrated on one another; chatting whenever their jog dwindled down to simply walking on the seashore. Most of the days, Mudit drove over to her bungalow on his motorbike and they left jogging together; he returning with her to have his morning cup of coffee at the Sanyals' house.

It was a good thing that none of the other Sanyals were up at that time of the morning, or Krish might have had something to say about Dipika's boyfriend who could not seem to stop touching her. Nor could Mudit control the heated glances he kept giving her. Not that Dipika was any less. She encouraged his touches, taking his hand in hers at every opportunity or kissing him whenever she felt like it, which appeared to be like all the time.

"Here." Dipika handed over a mug of coffee to Mudit who was sitting on a recliner in the garden room which caught the maximum sunlight in the mornings.

"Come here," he said, leaving his coffee mug on a table nearby and pointing to his lap.

Setting her own mug on the table, she sat down on his lap, smiling when he hugged her from behind. Leaning back, she settled comfortably against his chest, loving the feel of his muscular body against her slender back and his hard thighs beneath her own.

"Dippy…" He nuzzled her ear, taking a deep breath as he enjoyed her perfume, a touch of lemon and sandal and something which was unique to Dipika. "What's your plan for today?" he asked, tracing the shape of her ear with the tip of his tongue.

Her breath coming in gasps, she lifted his hands from her waist and placed them over her heaving breasts. It had been torture, these past few weeks, being in his proximity every morning and many times in the late evenings too. Not touching him had become more difficult each day. Right now, she was thrilled to be in his embrace, the only place she wanted to be. "Mmm…" she moaned when he squeezed her breasts, glorying in the sensation.

"You didn't answer my question," he said, shifting in the chair to ease his hardened shaft which was twitching beneath her curvy bottom.

"What question?" she asked, turning sideways before opening her slumberous eyes in a half slit to look up at him.

He gazed into her turbulent brown eyes, smiling when he noticed the desire in them. Leaning down to kiss one corner of her mouth, he said, "I asked you what your plan is for today."

That kiss had been too damn brief! Dipika opened her eyes wide to look at him. "Why don't you kiss me properly?"

"Are you sure we both know each other well enough?" came the swift response, a tad sarcastic. If the two weeks had been tough on her, they had been an absolute punishment for him. He forgot the number of cold showers he had taken each night before going to bed, sleep eluding him on most of them. He had taken a leaf out of her book and got into the habit of taking power naps; which was the only way he could keep his temper even.

"Mudit!" She pulled his face down to hers, kissing him on his mouth. "I'm sorry about that. I…" She could not speak further as her lips were crushed in a deep kiss as he explored her mouth thoroughly, as if it was the last kiss they would ever share.

It was a long while before he lifted his mouth from hers and studied her lovely face, her eyes barely open a slit while her luscious lips were parted even as her breaths came in gasps. His gaze moved down to her breasts, smiling when he noticed the hardened tips thrusting against the thin material of her t-shirt, despite the sports bra she was wearing. He stroked his thumbs over the distended nipples, smiling some more when she moaned hungrily. "Are you going to answer me at all?" he asked, kissing a soft cheek. It was Sunday and he was hoping they could spend the day together.

Dipika grimaced. "I have an event from four to seven and a party following that. Do you want to go with me?"

Mudit took a deep breath, doing his best to calm down his libido. Did he really want to watch her in her sexy clothes, as she spent time with her clients and their partners? He would only be able to see but not touch. It would be so damn frustrating.

Dipika could easily read his thoughts. Thinking quickly on her feet, she said, "Tell you what?"

"What?" There was a mutinous thrust to his square chin as he gave her a sharp glance, not sure if he was going to like what she was going to suggest.

She reached up to kiss the cleft in his chin, giving him a winning smile. "I'm begging you, Mudit," she whispered close to his ear, "will you make love to me?"

"What?" He pushed her off his lap to jump to his feet. "Now?"

She fluttered her eyelashes at him, her fists on her hips. "Does that mean a yay or a nay?"

"Yay, definitely," he growled, glaring down at her from his great height. "But..." he shook his head. He did not want her brother to murder him.

"Give me five minutes and I'll pack everything I need. And we can go over to your place. I..."

"Yes!" He pumped a fist in the air before lifting her up into his arms. "Yes, yes and yes."

Dipika threw back her head and laughed at his enthusiastic response.

"What's going on?" asked Krish, stepping into the garden room, a steaming cup of coffee in his hand, his right eyebrow raised quizzically.

"Dippy agreed to spend the day with me," said Mudit, giving his friend a wary look. "Is there more of that brew? I could use some." The coffee Dipika had brought earlier had gone cold.

"I thought you were agreeing to something she said, so vociferously too." Krish turned to look at his sister's blushing face and smiled.

"Mind your own business, Krish," said Dipika. Turning to Mudit, she offered, "I'll get coffee for both of us."

"What were you guys doing letting the coffee grow cold?" asked Krish, turning his gaze to Mudit.

"Ignore him, Mudit," suggested Dipika as she walked out of the room.

"Should I ask you about your intentions towards my sister?" asked Krish, faking a frown as he looked at Mudit.

"Maybe you should ask your sister what her intentions are towards me. If you haven't noticed, let me tell you, the lady calls all the shots."

Krish slapped a hand on Mudit's shoulder and roared with laughter, knowing fully well what Mudit must be undergoing. Dipika did like to get her own way. "I hear you man, I hear you. All I can do is wish you all the luck."

Dipika heard the tail end of his sentence when she entered the garden room. "Why does he need all the luck?" she asked Krish, pinning him with her sharp gaze.

Krish shrugged. "Just."

"Didn't I just tell you to mind your own business?" she asked, clenching her right hand in a fist as she got ready to punch her brother.

Krish placed his empty coffee mug down on a side table before lifting both his hands in front of his chest in a gesture of defence. "Chill, she-cat. I'm not saying anything. Ask Mudit if you want."

When she turned to Mudit, he walked forward to throw his arm around her waist. "Chill, babe. Krish didn't say anything objectionable. Now finish your coffee and go pack. We need to go."

Noticing the hot desire in his deep grey eyes, Dipika stopped arguing to gulp down her coffee and rushed to her room to pack an overnight case with three changes of clothing and her sexiest lingerie. She could not stop smiling when she thought of spending the next few hours in Mudit's bed, in his arms.

Mudit stood back against the wall, a glass of sparkling wine in his hand as he gazed at the people gathered in the grand ballroom of The Lalit, a five-star hotel not far from the international airport. The beauty pageant put together by some of the top model agencies in the country had been a supreme success. And Dipika, as the head of Amber Modelling Agency, was basking in its glory as she chatted with several people from the fashion industry.

A soft smile stretched across his face as he couldn't help recalling the time they had spent in his bed that very morning...

It had not taken long for Dipika to pack a small suitcase before she came into the garden where he was waiting beside his motorbike. There was something to be appreciated about a woman who was punctual. Especially considering the way Tanvi had kept him waiting every time he took her out. Once Dipika was settled on the back seat, he gunned the motor to race towards his bungalow, keen to get her into his bed.

And this time, he was not going to give her a chance to change her mind. And yes, he was going to shut off his cell phone first.

Dipika held on to him tightly, her hands locked over his flat abdomen and her face pressed to his broad back. She was thrilled to finally have decided to make love with him. It had not been easy waiting for two weeks, but she had not been sure how to approach him. Mudit inviting her to sit on his lap had made it easy for her. And she was not really worried about what her brother might say. Krish should not be saying anything. After all, had he not made love to Sanjana when they both were veritable strangers? He had even made her pregnant in the bargain. Dipika grinned to herself as she thought of the two of them, happily married now.

"I hope you haven't changed your mind." Mudit stopped the bike to turn towards her.

"No way. I can't wait to get my hands on you." She leaned forward to whisper in his ear.

"Good." His heart thundered, knocking against his rib-cage even as his blood pumped heavily through his veins. Getting off the bike, he lifted her suitcase in his right hand before gathering her close to his side with his left arm. "Don't let Kishore Uncle drag you into a conversation," he told her in a whisper.

Dipika giggled, looking up at him sideways. "I'll try not to."

"Nope." He shook his head firmly. "Trying doesn't help. Just don't stop to talk."

"Fine." She giggled some more. "Where's your room?"

"On the first floor. And no one dares to step in unless by invitation."

"Hmm."

"Good morning, Mudit, Dipika. Let me serve you coffee in the library."

"Good morning, Uncle. I've had two coffees from morning. Nothing for me," said Dipika, continuing to walk in the direction Mudit was guiding her.

"Same here, Uncle. We'll have lunch. In the meanwhile, we have some work to do. Please make sure we aren't disturbed."

Dipika could not stop giggling as she leaned against his shoulder, biting her lip to stop making a sound. Her eyes danced when they met Mudit's as they climbed up the wooden staircase to the left side of the main hall.

The moment they entered his room on the right, he threw the suitcase in one corner before tickling her mercilessly.

"Stop, stop please." Dipika laughed helplessly, unable to control herself as he tickled her extra sensitive waist.

"That's right, beg some more."

"Mudit, please," she gasped, falling back on the bed, trying to catch hold of his hands.

"Please what?" he asked, grinning down at her as his hands paused to caress her silky skin.

The giggle stuck in her throat when Dipika's pulse soared at his gentle touch on her sensitised skin. Gulping, she stared up at him with her gaze gone wide. "Love me?" she invited, her voice a hoarse whisper.

"With pleasure," he said, leaning down to stroke the tip of his tongue over the heavily beating pulse at her throat. The slightly salty taste of her skin drove him mad with hunger as he gathered her into his arms, cradling her against his chest.

Dipika tugged the hem of his t-shirt from his shorts, running her hands over his skin, roughened with short curls at the front and a satiny finish at the back. "I like touching you," she said, turning her face to his. "Kiss me, Mudit." She pouted her lips at him invitingly.

He pulled off his t-shirt and threw it behind him and with a growl of hunger, swooped down to take her mouth in his, tugging it open with his teeth before thrusting his tongue deeply within.

With a soft sigh of surrender, she drew his tongue into her mouth and sucked on it hungrily, mewling like a kitten as the kiss only made her crave for more.

Coming up for air after a long time, Mudit reached with shaky hands to pull her t-shirt over her head before throwing it behind him, gazing avidly at her heaving breasts as she took deep breaths. Cupping his large hands over her bounty, he squeezed them gently, smiling when she gasped in response. "Like it?"

She nodded, lifting herself above the bed before reaching behind to unhook her bra. "I'm all yours."

"As I'm yours," he said, tugging her bra straps down her shoulders before pulling it completely off her, his gaze never leaving her upper body. "You look so gorgeous," he declared in a rough voice, his vocal cords gone dry with longing. He cupped the underside of her breasts, stroking the soft tips with his thumbs. He smiled when her nipples responded eagerly by tightening into stiff buds. Leaning down, he stroked the left tip with his tongue, smiling some more when he heard her moan.

Dipika placed her hands over the sides of his head, her fingers digging into his scalp even as she pushed her body closer to his tantalising mouth.

Turning his head, he caressed the other nipple, inadvertently brushing his unshaven jaw against the plump flesh.

She almost jumped off the bed when she felt his bristly cheek scrape against the soft flesh of her breast, moaning in ecstasy. "Mmm…" she hummed when he took the turgid nipple into his mouth and suckled on it greedily.

Not caring for the lovemaking to be over even before it began, Mudit threw a muscular leg over both of hers as she wriggled wildly under him, making him almost come apart. "Patience, babe."

"Noooo… now," she demanded, her hands at his back, her nails digging into the muscles, totally unaware of the marks she was leaving on him as she took a bite of his shoulder.

He groaned, even more aroused than he already was because of the wild nature of the woman in his arms. "Dippy…" He reached down to open the button of her denim shorts before sliding it down her hips along with her lace panties.

The impatient Dipika kicked her legs, trying to get rid of her shorts and panties.

"Whoa! Easy woman. Are you trying to unman me?" he growled, getting up on his knees to help her out of her garments.

"Eh?" She stared up at his face, her hands pressed to his flat abdomen. "Did I do something wrong?" she asked.

"No, you wild cat, you did nothing wrong," he teased, getting off the bed to remove his own shorts, his eyes studying her expressive face avidly.

Her breathing erratic, she watched the strip show as he pushed down his shorts, his swollen manhood coming into view as it appeared like a large finger pointing accusingly at her. "Ooh!"

"What?" he asked, fully aware of the impressive figure he cut, his powerful thighs trembling with the pressure he felt of taking it slow. After all, it was their first time together and he wanted it to be a good, no, great one.

"Come to me." Her voice was a command as she threw open her arms invitingly.

And he went. Lying down across her body, Mudit gently parted her legs. At least, he tried to be as gentle as he could under the circumstances, before wrapping them around his waist. He reached down with a forefinger to check if she was ready for him, pleased to find her throbbing wetness. Taking a deep breath, he rose above her to place the tip of his penis at the entrance to her vagina. "Ready?" he asked, his voice gruff with sudden emotion, his eyes glowing as they looked deeply into hers.

"Oh yes!" she said, her voice a soft sigh as she spread her hands on his chest, her palms rubbing over his flat male nipples in a caress. "Pleasssse…" she begged, moaning loudly when she felt him thrust into her.

And he entered her in a single stroke, settling inside with a grunt. Oh, it felt so damn good, sheathed inside her womb, the fit so snug and tight. He leaned down to take her mouth in a scorching kiss, his hands planted firmly on the bed on both sides of her.

"Mudit…" she moaned once he let go of her mouth to trail a chain of kisses along her jaw.

"Babe…" He pulled out of her slowly before pushing in once again; continuing to pull and push even as he increased the pace until both of them were gasping for breath.

The few times Dipika had had sex with her only boyfriend had never brought her to orgasm. Just now, with Mudit pumping deeply into her even as he suckled her breasts in turn, she felt herself being lifted higher and higher, her hands clutching at the sheets as if that would help anchor her body to the earth. But no, her body was determined to spin off into space even as she completely lost control over it, her head whirling ecstatically. It was an effort to breathe as Mudit was relentless in riding her, not pausing for even an instant.

His jaw felt rock hard as he drove into her repeatedly, willing her to climax as he was on the verge of breaking apart at any moment.

"Aaaaaah…" Dipika screamed at the top of her voice as she came apart in his arms, her body shuddering in the aftermath of a powerful orgasm, her first ever. She shook her head from side to side, her hands clutching at his shoulders, tearing up at the incredible sensation shaking up her whole body.

"Dippyyyyyy…" He followed right behind, coming longer and harder than he had ever had before, finally flopping over her supine body, having no strength to move away.

Dipika hugged him close, refusing to let go, loving his weight on her satiated body, her hands gently stroking his trembling back. "That was simply amazing," she whispered against his neck.

He laughed softly somewhere above her head, murmuring, "Wasn't it?" before promptly falling asleep.

Mudit suddenly became aware of his surroundings as if he had just woken up from a deep sleep where he was having a wonderful dream. A smile softened his rugged features as he pierced a piece of *paneer kabab* on a toothpick a passing waiter offered him. Popping the starter into his mouth, he munched on it, relishing the burst of flavours which hit his senses.

"Which brands do you model for?" asked the woman who walked up to him just then, her keen gaze studying his face avidly.

"Eh?" He turned to look at the skimpily dressed woman who was probably in her forties, and lifted an eyebrow in query.

"You are a model, right?" she said, giving him a wide smile, confident that she was correct.

"Wrong," he said, lifting his wine glass to take a sip, grimacing at the taste. It was excellent quality, but just that he was not much of a wine drinker; more of the whisky kind. Placing the flute on the tray another waiter was carrying, he turned towards the bar, stopping when he felt the woman's hand on his arm. "What?" he asked, not really caring that he was being rude.

"Who are you?" she asked, stepping a little too close for comfort.

What the fuck!

His first instinct was to tell her to get lost. Controlling his temper with an effort, he looked down his hawk-like nose at the stranger. "I am Mudit Trivedi," he responded briefly.

She watched his face with a small scowl of concentration, a finger on her lower lip. "I haven't heard of you."

He shrugged.

"Oh, by the way, I am Niranjana Sabharwal," she said, seeming to suddenly realise that she had not introduced herself.

"Nice to meet you, ma'am," he said. "Should I get you something to drink?" he asked as an afterthought, his good manners kicking in automatically.

Niranjana was baffled. Did he not know who she was? She frowned up at him. She was the head of a Bollywood production house and people from the modelling industry were ready to give an arm and a leg to make her acquaintance. And here she was, trying to get to know this hunk; and look at the way he was behaving, as if he did not give a damn about it. But then, she was not to know that Mudit was simply not interested in the fashion industry; or at least, only to the limit of how it affected his girlfriend's life.

Thinking quickly on her feet, she said, "Get me a Bloody Mary with an extra dash of vodka."

That verged on an order and he did not like it one bit. Making an effort to keep the scowl off his face, Mudit gave her a brief nod before walking up to the bar. It took a while to get the two orders—whisky with soda for himself and the vodka cocktail for Niranjana Sabharwal—before he returned to where he had been standing earlier. It did not matter that he did not know anyone here. Mudit enjoyed watching people and never felt lonely.

"Here you go, Niranjana," he said, handing the cocktail glass to the woman who was by now surrounded by a number of young people, both men and women. Good! Now that she had company, she would probably leave him alone. Lifting his hand in a wave, Mudit turned to walk away only to be once again stopped in his tracks by her hand on his arm.

What the hell!

"Did you want something else? Maybe I can find a waiter to help you," he offered, half sarcastic.

Niranjana, who was renowned for her quick and fiery temper which came with the power she wielded in her field, took a deep breath to retain a semblance of calm. It was obvious that Mudit Trivedi did not know who she was and it was time that he did. "Listen, I don't think you know who I am. I…"

"But I do. Only a few minutes ago you mentioned you were Niranjana Sabharwal." His voice was impatient as he responded to her before taking a swig of his whisky, glad that it was of excellent quality. "Unless you think I should have recognised your name?" There was a question in his voice as he looked down at the diminutive woman whose head barely reached up to his shoulder.

Several gasps were heard the moment Mudit uttered those words, obviously having shocked the youngsters who had been hanging around the woman. He turned to look around him, feeling kind of trapped. Had he made a *faux pas*? Why were they all staring at him as if he had said something offensive? He returned his gaze to Niranjana, an eyebrow up in query.

She shook her head at him. "What the hell are you doing here at this party? Have you gate crashed?" she asked, her voice a snarl, even as sparks flew from her angry gaze.

Why me? Mudit looked at her askance. He had been standing in a corner—the very corner she was occupying now, along with a number of tittering fools who seemed to be hanging on to her every word— all by himself. It was she who had approached him and introduced herself. And now she was offended all because he had not recognised who she was. Well, Mudit did not know all that much about the modelling industry. He had enjoyed the show earlier in the evening. Like any red-blooded male, he had admired the beautiful women clad in dazzling clothes. Of course, there had been many male models too. And they had looked awesome as well. But that was the extent of his interest. Who the hell was this Sabharwal woman who appeared all set to throw him out of the party?

"I don't really think it's any of your business," he responded, his voice turning cold enough to freeze a whole river. He lifted his glass and downed the half glass of whisky before turning away from her, or at least tried to.

"Wait a minute here," she commanded, her hand once again on his arm.

While he had a good mind to knock her hand off, he retained his patience to stop in his tracks. "What now?"

"How did you get inside?" she asked, her voice commanding as she glared up at him.

"Mudit is my guest," said a cool voice as Dipika stepped forward to tuck her arm into his, her brown eyes glowing with temper. She had been watching the scene from across the ballroom over the past few minutes, doing her best to go to Mudit's rescue even as she was stopped on her way by so many of the guests who were keen to greet her. Niranjana Sabharwal was a barracuda in Dipika's opinion. And how the woman had managed to get her teeth into Mudit was something she was keen to find out.

"Dipika Sanyal! Great show, I must say. Congratulations!" Niranjana's voice was sweetly poisonous as she glowered at her adversary. It was not as if they had a personal vendetta. But the fact was that Niranjana hated all women, especially successful ones like Dipika.

"Thanks. And if you will excuse us?" Dipika tried to prise Mudit away from the scene, only Niranjana was not yet ready to let him go.

"Your guest... he says he's not a model." The way Niranjana phrased her sentence, anybody would think that Mudit had been lying to her.

Dipika's eyes went wide in surprise before she lifted them to Mudit's face. She almost laughed when she saw the mischievous expression in his dancing grey eyes; his temper having disappeared the moment Dipika placed a hand on his arm. "That's right. He isn't."

"Then what is he?" Niranjana demanded to know. She just about managed not to stamp her foot in a temper as she glared at the two of them.

"I am a boring accountant," said Mudit, tongue firmly tucked in his cheek.

"What?" The word was a shout as Niranjana's eyes almost popped out of her skull. "I refuse to believe it."

He shrugged. "You are free to believe whatever you want, ma'am." Turning to Dipika, he asked, "Do you wanna dance?"

"Yes, please." They walked away before Niranjana could stop them.

"Who the hell is she?" asked Mudit as he led Dipika to the dancing area, an arm around her slender waist.

Dipika laughed. "Are you aware that you locked horns with a notorious Bollywood producer? She eats men like you for breakfast." She continued to laugh up into his handsome face.

"She does? Ugh! My offending her... is it going to affect you or your business in some way?"

Dipika shook her head. "Nope. But she is trouble with a capital T. It's best to stay clear of her."

He grimaced. "I was standing all by myself when she approached me, asking which brands I modelled for."

"Aah!" Dipika looked up into his handsome face. "Then I suppose I can't really blame the woman." She went on tiptoes to kiss him on his cheek which was already rough with a few hours of stubble. After all, he had only shaved that morning, before tumbling her on his bed for the second time.

"Et tu Brute." He quoted Shakespeare's Julius Caesar as he gave her a mock glare, grinning when she burst out laughing.

"I'm sorry I left you alone among a pack of wolves," she said, her voice continuing to shake with laughter.

"She-wolves," he grumbled, nuzzling her ear. "By the way, thanks for the wonderful romp in bed. It was an amazing experience. Did you enjoy yourself?" he asked. She had been in a tearing rush soon after the second round and they had not had a chance to talk about it.

Dipika's eyes turned sultry as she looked up into his heated gaze. "Too much. And I want more of it." She pressed her body close to his chest. Neither of them cared that the DJ was playing a fast number as they moved their feet languorously, even as they clung to one another.

"When can you leave?" he asked eagerly, kissing her silky cheek. After all, it was past eleven and she had been working from two in the afternoon.

"In about an hour?"

He groaned softly. "That long?"

"Why?" she asked, fluttering her eyelashes at him mischievously.

"I can't wait to make love to you again," he growled, capturing her lips in a scorching kiss, glad that the light had turned dim in the dancing area.

"Don't tempt me," said Dipika when they came up for air, her lips wet and quivering from the assault of his kiss. "Just one hour, I promise."

His hands on her hips, Mudit pulled her close to his lower body, hoping to ease the pressure on his tumescent shaft. "Are you going to leave me stranded on the dance floor?" he asked, lifting an eyebrow at her.

She laughed softly, shaking her head from side to side. "As head of my agency, I have already set a number of people to finish the work. I just need to be here so that my presence is felt."

"In other words, you can entertain me while we wait for the work to get done." He winked at her, mighty pleased that he need not part company with her.

She pulled his head down to whisper in his ear, "I'm not really surprised that Niranjana Sabharwal was trying to get your attention; so desperately too."

"And why would that be?" he asked, his eyes crinkling at the corners as he turned his gaze to look deeply into hers.

"Are you even aware how sexy you appear this evening?" No, she did not blame Niranjana, not at all. And she was thrilled that this man was hers, and hers alone, at least for now.

"You mean in my three-piece suit?" he asked, wiggling his eyebrows.

She burst out laughing. "Well, I was thinking in terms of stripping you of each garment slowly and torturously before the night is out."

He groaned softly. "Believe me, babe, your words are enough to kill me," he muttered, kissing the pulse at her throat.

8

Mudit was glad when the directors' meeting finally came to a close. Just as he was getting up from his chair, Arjun gestured for him to wait. Once the rest of the people exited the board room, Arjun walked forward to sit on the chair right next to Mudit's.

"What's bugging you?" he asked his friend, eyeing him keenly.

"Is it so obvious?" asked Mudit, grimacing.

Arjun smiled. "Probably only to me. Come on, spit it out. Is it Dip who is giving you trouble?"

A sudden smile lit up Mudit's face as he shook his head slowly from side to side. "Dippy is the one who's keeping me happy and sane these days." While her family and friends called her Dip, Mudit himself preferred the version little Kabir had for his aunt, and called her Dippy.

"And who is making you unhappy?" asked the shrewd Arjun.

A huge sigh shuddered through Mudit's being. "*Arre yaar*, it's my parents. They have been asking me to go home to Surat for a long time. But," he shrugged, "I just can't. I will hate it there, I know. Even the thought of a trip to Surat makes me feel claustrophobic, to be truthful."

"Hmm." Arjun was well aware of Mudit's feelings towards his parents and did not have an opinion regarding it. He did not really blame Mudit for wanting to stay away from his immediate family.

"And now, they have fixed Bhoomi's engagement and marriage; both functions to be held in the span of a week. Imagine! We Gujjus generally prefer a long engagement period. But this seems to be a unique situation and that's why they have organised it the way they have. The engagement is on March 19 and the wedding set for March 26." He grimaced some more. "And they have a whole lot of ceremonies in between. I simply cannot imagine being stuck there for eight whole days. But then again, there's no escape from it." And there was the point that he was going to miss Dipika, terribly. His parents had told him all about the wedding arrangements only the earlier evening and as there was still a month to go for the marriage, he was in no hurry to speak about it to her.

"Ouch!" Arjun placed a pacifying hand on Mudit's shoulder. "Rather you than me," he said in commiseration.

"Oh, and there's something else. They have found the perfect woman for me, it seems. They plan to set up a meeting with her. I know I get to reject her. But even then, it's so damn embarrassing. I cannot believe that my family is still living in the last century." Mudit wanted to smash something. Even after repeatedly telling them that he was not interested in meeting this *sanskari chhokri* they had chosen for him, his mother had been insistent. "Just meet her once, *na*, Mudit. You don't have to marry her if you do not like," was what she had told him over the call last evening.

Now that was going to be awkward for Mudit—meeting a girl without the intention of even considering her for marriage.

Arjun shook his head, thinking for a few moments. He snapped his fingers suddenly and said, "Why don't you take Dip along with you? It might solve all your problems."

"But... but I don't know if I want to marry Dippy. I..."

"So, who's asking you to marry her?" asked Arjun.

"That's the impression my people will have if I take her along with me; even presuming she can take more than a week off from her business." He had seen how Dipika tended to work even on Sundays at times. She was completely dedicated to the business she had set up and thoroughly enjoyed what she was doing. "And taking her to my home, what if Dippy gets the wrong idea? That I plan to propose marriage?" Mudit was totally confused. Arjun's idea sounded good on the surface; maybe great even. But it could create a number of complications later. Damn it all!

"You don't really owe anything to your folks, do you? Let them think what they want. They..."

"And how do I introduce Dippy to them? That she's my fuck buddy?" Mudit asked, highly sarcastic.

Arjun threw back his head and laughed out loud. "I can imagine your mother and father's faces when you do that."

Mudit's frown disappeared to be replaced by a smile which soon broadened into a grin. "Help me, *yaar*, Arjun."

"I am trying to, if only you will listen fully. If you take Dip with you, and introduce her as your girlfriend—no more and no less—then your problem of meeting this *sanskari chhokri* is sorted." Arjun could not help grinning as he quoted the words which Mudit had mentioned to him earlier. "And you can book yourself into a hotel not too far away from your house and your family gets no whiff of your sleeping arrangements. What say?"

"Brilliant!" Mudit jumped to his feet and pulled Arjun up to give him a hug. "You are my best buddy, *yaar*."

Arjun laughed. "Glad to be of help, as long as you realise I am your "best" buddy and not the other kind," he teased, drawing quotes with his fingers when he mentioned best as against fuck.

"Very funny," said Mudit, giving his friend a mock glare. "Now, all I have to do is persuade Dippy that I'm taking her out on a vacay…"

"To meet all the members of your family," declared Arjun, tongue firmly tucked in his cheek, even as his eyes glinted mischievously.

"You are going to be the death of me, man. I'd better go before you drive me crazy. But thanks for the idea. It's definitely worth trying."

"Any time, bro."

It was past midnight when Dipika drove into Mudit's compound and parked her car at the side, next to his Audi. She was wide awake despite the lateness of the hour and could not wait to cuddle in his arms. He was not only an intelligent conversationalist but also a generous lover and she thoroughly enjoyed every moment she spent with Mudit.

A man worth keeping for ever? She was seriously considering it.

She let herself into the bungalow with the spare key he had given her, glad that she would not have to come across Kishorilal. Somehow, she was convinced that the old man disapproved of her relationship with Mudit. Well, after all, Mudit had never brought any of his girlfriends home before now.

Which, again, gave her a lot of hope and promise.

"Dippy." Mudit stepped out of the library when he heard the front door open, smiling when his gaze fell upon Dipika shutting the door. He opened his arms wide and was pleased when she rushed into them. "Miss me?" he asked, kissing her forehead.

"Always." She threw her arms around his naked torso as he was clad only in a pair of boxers. "You look hot, dude," she said, looking up into his face.

Colour ran over his rugged cheeks as he grinned down at her. "Not as hot as you do, babe." He ran his hand down her bare thighs, glad for the short dress she was wearing. "Busy day?"

"Mmm... give me a kiss."

He pressed his open mouth to her cheek, tracing the line of her jaw with the tip of his tongue before nibbling one corner of her mouth.

Dipika turned her face to capture his lips only for him to move away before kissing her neck. "Mudit…"

"Hmm…" He pushed the sleeveless strap of her dress out of the way as he pressed brief, but heated kisses down the slope of her shoulder.

"That's how you are going to play, are you?" she growled before placing her hand over his manhood, running her hand up and down his length in a caress. She grinned when she felt him growing bigger and harder under her firm strokes.

"Dippy…" he sighed, pressing himself into her wandering hand. "That feels so good, babe."

She abruptly took her hand off to look up at him, smiling when she saw the rapturous expression on his face, his eyes shut firmly, his short curly eyelashes pressing down on his lean manly cheeks. She smiled when he suddenly opened his eyes to look down at her.

"Why did you stop?"

"I'm waiting for your kiss," she said, pouting at him, giggling when he suddenly lifted her up into his arms to throw her over his left shoulder and walked towards the staircase. "Caveman," she declared, continuing to giggle.

"I'll show you caveman," he declared, throwing her down in the centre of his bed before jumping over her.

The giggles froze in her throat when he took her mouth in a fiery kiss.

It was only much later in the morning when Mudit got a chance to speak to Dipika about his forthcoming Surat trip. They had been jogging for thirty minutes before they slowed down to a walk down the beach. Taking her hand in his, he said, "Listen, I need a favour from you."

"Favour?" She turned to gaze into his deep grey eyes, surprised on hearing the word from him. "Anything. Tell me."

"Hear me out before making any promises," he said, a warning note in his voice.

"Oh my, this seems serious," said Dipika, half-teasing as she stopped in her tracks to stand facing him.

"It is," he sighed, still not clear how to broach the subject without her reading more into it than what he wanted her to.

She looked up at his profile as he was half turned towards the calm sea, the sunlight brightening up the side of his face facing her. *Oh God, but he is handsome,* she thought, her heart beating loudly within her chest. Dipika suddenly realised that she could not imagine her life without Mudit; a man she had met barely a month ago. Imagine that! *What did he want from her?* "Mudit?"

He turned to his right to gaze down at Dipika's lovely face. "I need to visit my family. My sister is getting married and they want me there."

"Oh! Okay. When is the wedding?" She hoped he was not going for a long visit. She would miss him terribly anyway, whether it was one day or ten.

He sighed loudly, a deep frown bringing his thick eyebrows together. "That's the issue. The ceremonies begin with an engagement and end with the wedding, all set from one Sunday to the next."

"You will be gone for all of eight days?" she asked, her eyes going wide with shock. She wondered if she had enough work to bury herself in, the whole of twenty-four-seven. She was sure she was not going to be able to sleep a wink during the time he was away.

He gave her a pathetic glance. "Yes." Thinking on his feet, he decided to come clean. "Listen, I told you I needed a favour."

"Hmm." What could she do? Dipika could not think of anything.

"I want you to go with me, for two reasons." He stopped, waiting to know her reaction.

Mudit was taking her to meet his family. Dipika could not believe her ears even as her heart soared. Colour rushing over her cheeks, she looked up at him with shining eyes. Her excitement dimmed when she noticed the lack of smile on his face. He did not look like a man proposing marriage; or even one who was seriously considering it. And he had, not one, but two reasons for taking her to his home town. Her excitement completely draining out of her, she said, "Go on."

"My parents have found a suitable woman for me to marry and are keen to set up a meeting. I have no intention of being married in the near future, that too, to a stranger. I…"

"But she won't be a stranger when you get to know her," protested Dipika. She could not help wondering at her own sanity. Had she just now encouraged him to meet a strange woman, considering her for a life partner? She felt a strange pressure in her chest, as if her heart was hurting.

He frowned heavily. "Are you trying to push me into a strange woman's arms?" he growled, glaring at her.

She shrugged. "If that's what you want."

"It's you I want, and you very well know it." It was an effort to not shout the words at her, not out here on the beach with so many people within hearing distance.

A small smile broke out on Dipika's face. But she was still irritated with him. Only, she did not know how to voice her feelings. "For how long?" she asked instead.

"As long as it takes," he growled, leaning down to capture her mouth in a torrid kiss. "Let me be frank, Dipika. I have never felt the depth of feeling towards anyone, what I feel for you. But then again, I'm not ready for marriage. I…"

She placed a trembling hand over his mouth to stop him from speaking further. Giving him a relieved smile, she said, "I am glad that you are being upfront here. I'm not ready for marriage either. And I like you a lot." Her smile widened into a grin. "We need time with each other."

"Exactly." Phew! Was he glad they both were on the same page. "Now, about my parents…"

"You need a woman by your side, to keep your parents off your back. At the same time, you don't want this woman to read too much into your gesture of taking her to meet your parents."

Highly relieved, he gave her a wide grin. "That's it in a nutshell."

"I'm your woman," she said, reaching up to press her mouth to his in a brief kiss.

"Dippy, babe! You are the best. Can you take a break for eight days at a stretch?" he asked.

"It depends on the sleeping arrangements," she said, giving him a saucy grin.

"Hahaha!" He threw back his head and laughed out loud, feeling so light for the first time after he received the news of his sister's wedding. "Which brings me to the second reason why I want you to accompany me. I cannot imagine not making love to you for eight days." He tucked his arm into hers before turning her in the direction of home.

"I cannot do that either, which brings me back to the sleeping arrangements. I…"

"I'm booking a hotel suite for both of us, not far from my family home. I just needed your confirmation before doing it."

"I plan to work every day, okay?"

"As do I," he said, hugging her. "Babe, you are the best thing to happen to me in decades," he declared passionately, kissing her temple.

"Do we have time for a quick roll in the bed before taking off for the day?" she asked, her voice a sexy purr.

"Most definitely, yes," he agreed, giving her a wolfish grin.

"*Mudit na Pappa!*" Sharda rushed down the staircase to meet her husband just as he entered the hall of their bungalow.

"What are you excited about?" asked Chandulal, staring at his wife's animated face in surprise.

"Mudit called to say that he is coming." She jumped from one foot to the other, too thrilled with the idea of seeing her son after so many years. The last time they had met him was during the death rites of Shiamak Trivedi, his grandfather, and Chandulal's father, three years ago.

Being the younger son, Shiamak had moved to Mumbai to make his living, leaving behind his wife and son Chandulal, in Surat. The two of them had lived with Shiamak's father and elder brother and his wife. The bungalow had passed into Chandulal's hands when his elder uncle had died without leaving behind an offspring. Chandulal's standard of living also improved thanks to his father to begin with, and later his son Mudit. Now, he and his other two sons earned well, more than enough to lead a grand lifestyle, having renovated the bungalow in the latest trend.

Curbing his happiness at the news, Chandulal asked, "When is he coming?"

"On the morning of the engagement."

"He must have the best room, you understand?" said the father, wiping his hands on the towel she offered before sitting down on the swing to relish the snacks and tea Sharda had placed on a stool nearby.

"Yes, yes. I was thinking the corner room on the right side. What do you say?"

The bungalow had a large central hall with two doors on the left and two on the right on the ground floor. One led to the kitchen and dining area, a second to the *puja* room, on the left. On the right, there were two bedrooms, one belonging to Chandulal and his wife and the other used as a guest room.

The first floor also had a main hall and six bedrooms, with two verandas which ran around the house, on both the ground floor and the first floor. While three rooms were occupied by their children Arvind, Dinesh and Bhoomi, the other three bedrooms were spare. The two corner bedrooms were the largest and caught the maximum breeze.

"You know best," he finally agreed, looking forward to spending time with his eldest son, who seemed like a stranger more than ever.

Arvind, Dinesh and Bhoomi had by now joined their parents in the hall. Arvind was the second son, three years younger to Mudit at twenty-nine. Next in line was Dinesh, aged twenty-six. Bhoomi was the youngest at twenty-three. They were all graduates. While the brothers had trained at diamond cutting and worked with some of the top jewellers in Surat, Bhoomi had no choice but to remain at home, waiting for the right man to come along and marry her. That way, both Chandulal and Sharda were in total agreement that a woman's place was in her husband's household. Neither of them believed in a career for a woman. Sitting at home, twiddling her thumbs while watching TV serials, had made Bhoomi a grumpy young lady. Finally, she was glad that she was to be married soon, to Roopak Kandoi, who ran a silk sari manufacturing unit along with his father. Being an only son, he was to get the whole business—the monthly turnover running into crores of rupees—handed solely over to him when his father retired. Bhoomi could not wait to be free of her dull existence as the youngest child of the Trivedis.

While the three siblings had heard a lot about Mumbai and the high-flying lives people led there, they had never had a chance to visit the metropolis. Neither had their oldest brother invited them over to stay with him, nor did their parents encourage them to go over. None of the three were clear about the relationship Mudit had with his family. So much so that Arvind resented the way his parents eagerly awaited their eldest child's visit to the family home.

"When is Mudit coming?" asked Dinesh, asking the question which was topmost in the minds of all three siblings.

"On Sunday morning," said Sharda, an expression of abject delight on her face. It was not as if she loved Mudit more than the other three children, but he was the one she had given up when he was barely twelve. The menfolk had not been bothered that they were breaking her heart when they sent him away.

After all, she had three other children to love and take care of.

Dinesh's face darkened with jealous thoughts. Why did his mother love Mudit so much more than she did him? She was ever so excited that Mudit was coming home. Did Arvind and Dinesh not count? Was it because Mudit was richer than they were? Or smarter? He turned to give his brother a corner-eyed glance and was satisfied to see a similar expression of disgruntlement on his sibling's face.

"Your mother is getting the corner room ready for him, the one on the right side. I hope you both will help her set it up as soon as possible." Chandulal looked at his two sons with a stern expression on his face. But then, that was how the father was, not really knowing how to smile. He had carried too heavy a burden on his shoulders as the father of not one, not two, but four children. It had been a tremendous relief when his own father had offered to take charge of bringing up Mudit, who was growing out of his clothes every six months. And he seemed to eat enough food to feed a whole household. While he had been aware that his wife was not really happy about sending her eldest child away, Chandulal had had no choice but to grab the opportunity when it presented itself.

"I have been asking you to give me that corner room for so long. But you always said no." Dinesh's blood boiled with anger and jealousy. Arvind had the corner room on the left and was damned chuffed about it. Dinesh had always coveted the room at the other corner, but both his parents had refused to let him have it. And now, it looked like the prodigal son was the lucky one.

"Shh, Dinesh. It is Mudit's right as the eldest born," said his mother, placing a pacifying hand on his shoulder.

Dinesh shook her hand off, glaring at her, his eyes spitting fire. "But he doesn't even live here." It was an effort to keep his voice mild, but one simply could not get away with shouting, not in the Trivedi household. There was always the fear that they might be sent away, just as Mudit had been.

"Exactly. He's going to be here for eight days, or maybe nine at the most. He…"

"Will you let me have the room after he leaves?" asked Dinesh, determined to get his way. "After all, it might take another twenty years for Mudit to visit us again."

"How dare you say that?" There were angry tears in Sharda's eyes as she glared at her third son. "And here I was hoping he would visit us more often."

"On what basis do you think that's going to happen?" asked Arvind logically. He agreed with Dinesh that the latter should get the corner room at the right side of the house. After all, it was only the two of them who will be living in this house; especially now with Bhoomi going off to her husband's house after getting married.

"That's enough," said Chandulal, glaring at his sons. While he agreed with the boys, he did not want his wife to be hurt, not more than she already was. "Listen to what your mother says."

And that was that!

Dipika was exceptionally busy during the week preceding their trip to Surat as she had to organise a lot of things and delegate a number of tasks. Sanjana was totally supportive throughout the time.

"You don't worry about anything, Dip. Go on and have fun. I'm sure I can handle everything. And Krish can help out if it's really necessary."

"I know, Sanju. It's just that I don't want you guys to abandon Kabir and spend all your time doing the agency's work. But then again, I think everything is under control. All the models know their itinerary, and it's a good thing that there is no major event happening during those days. The smaller ones kind of take care of themselves. And you are a treasure, Sanju. I don't know how I would manage without you."

Colour rushed up Sanjana's cheeks at her sister-in-law-cum-boss's wholesome compliment. But more than anything, Dipika was her best friend, the one person who had been a great support when Sanjana had taken a leap of confidence and moved to Mumbai all the way from Johannesburg. "I'm sure you would have done well, as always." She knew Dipika to be the brilliant entrepreneur she was; her modelling agency being one of the topmost in the country.

They hugged each other before Dipika declared, "I think that's it. Now, I can take care of my packing. There is going to be at least five different ceremonies, I think. It's best if I'm prepared for all contingencies."

"I'm sure you'll rock it, Dip. My only bother is that you don't outshine the bride," laughed Sanjana, winking at her sister-in-law.

"Meh! *Kuch bhi.*"

The two of them sorted through Dipika's wardrobe before foraging through the many clothes which they stocked for photo shoots and put together a number of dresses with matching accessories for the trip to Surat. It was a good thing Mudit and she were driving over, or she would have had to pay a lot of excess baggage on a flight. By the time she was packed, Dipika had two large trolley cases full of clothes. "I hope Mudit isn't going to kill me," she muttered.

"Do you think he'll really notice the luggage when he is with you?" asked Sanjana cheekily.

Dipika grinned. "I know he's kind of enamoured with me, but he's a smart cookie and damned observant."

"I'm sure he's also aware that women need clothes of all kinds, especially for this kind of trip with ceremonies galore."

"I sure hope so."

As for Mudit, he was also working furiously, doing his best to complete as much as possible before leaving for the trip. While Dipika might have time to work, he was not too sure about himself as his family would be expecting him to spend a lot of time with them, especially his parents. Which was again working at the back of his mind, like a burr under the saddle, creating a constant irritation which made him moody.

"Hey!" Dipika called him at eight in the evening. "All set?"

"For what?" he growled, glaring at his laptop. Tucking his phone between his ear and shoulder, he rubbed both his hands over his eyes. "What are you so happy about?"

"Eh?" What was wrong? He sounded so irritated. "Is everything alright, Mudit?" she asked in a soothing voice.

"As much as it's ever going to be." He turned the power off before shutting his laptop.

"Are you still at work?"

"Yes. Just shutting my laptop, actually. How about you?"

"I'm all done. I packed too. And you?"

"Not even started yet," he muttered, pushing his laptop into its case along with the charger.

"Do you want me to help?" she asked. It was Friday evening and they were planning to leave mid-morning the next day to reach Surat by evening. It was a six-hour-long drive. With a few stops in between, it was only going to take longer.

"I would like you to do a lot of things for me," he said, his mood changing abruptly.

"Would you like me to give you a full body massage? You sound like you need one."

"That grumpy, huh?" he asked, grimacing when his manhood twitched in response to her offer.

"Worse," she declared, laughing.

"There's one part of me which needs your loving touch more than any other, babe. I can't wait to see you."

"Same here."

"Do you want me to pick you up on my way home?"

"That would be perfect. I'll see you soon." She blew him a kiss before disconnecting the call. She was pretty excited to go on the trip with Mudit. While she was aware that he was not too keen to visit his home town, she was hoping she could keep him in a happier frame of mind.

"Is this the lot of your luggage?" asked Mudit, picking up the first case to stash it into the boot of his car.

"You don't think it's too much?" she asked, a surprised expression on her face.

He gave her a grin. "Not at all. We are going away for more than a week. What with the engagement, wedding, etc, you will need a lot of stuff. And hey, I can help you dress up," he offered, shutting the boot to step towards her.

She pouted at him. "You think we will get anywhere on time that way?" she asked.

Cupping her cheek, he leaned down to steal a quick kiss. "I think we should begin practising, tonight itself."

She rolled her eyes at him before getting inside the car.

"Your offer to help me pack… were you serious?" he asked, driving out of the gates from the Sanyal home.

"Of course, yes."

"I suppose you do a lot of packing and unpacking."

She turned towards him to give him a wide grin. "I do the packing because I love it. It also feels good to be in control." She gave him a wink before continuing, "As for unpacking, that's why I employ others." She had two girls who were responsible for keeping all the clothes in excellent condition. The job also included unpacking.

"Hahaha! Smart lady, indeed." He took her hand in his to kiss the back. "And about the massage, is the offer still open?" he asked, stopping the car in his compound, and unbuckling his seat belt to turn towards her.

"Of course. It's more for me than for you," she said, her voice hoarse when she lifted her gaze to his.

He reached across to kiss her, long and hard. "That's my woman," he declared.

They had dinner first, before going up to his room. With a lot of interference and very little help from Mudit, Dipika managed to pack his clothes—Indian formal, western formal, smart casuals and regular wear. She packed three pairs of shoes, two sets of leather footwear, two pairs of *mojiris* and a whole lot of socks. "Mudit, do you have something to wear under this *kurta*? Some kind of an inner wear?" She lifted a brilliant white linen *kurta* to show him.

Mudit, who was working on his laptop, lifted his head to gaze at her and then the piece of garment in her hand. "I never wear anything under it. Do you think I might need something?" he asked.

"Not if you want to display your sexy torso to all the women there." She gave him a mocking glance before folding the garment and placing it inside the suitcase she was packing.

"You think my torso is sexy?" He was beside her the next instant, pulling her back to his bare chest, even as he bent down to nuzzle the curve of her cheek.

"Mudit." Dipika placed her hands over his where they lay against her flat stomach, trying to prise them away from her body. "Why don't you finish your work and allow me to complete mine?" she asked in a shaky voice when she felt him trailing his lips over the side of her neck.

"Work is boring!" he declared. "And I need the massage." He took her hand and placed it over the front of his shorts. "See?"

She cupped him in her hand before turning to face him. "Okay, a five-minute break. But that's all, okay?" She lifted her eyebrows in enquiry, waiting for him to agree to her condition.

"What do you plan to do in five minutes?" he asked curiously, excited to find out all about it. She could be an innovative lover, his Dipika.

"For that, you'll need to wait and watch. Do you agree?"

He gave a dramatic sigh. "As if I have a choice," he grumbled.

"Poor darling," she laughed, going down on her knees in front of him before quickly unbuttoning his shorts to pull them down the length of his muscular legs, scraping her nails over his sensitised skin deliberately. She smiled when his shaft twitched in response even as she heard him groan loudly.

"Are you planning to kill me, Dippy?" he asked, his voice a growl of need.

"Only with pleasure," she insisted before closing her lips over the tip of his manhood. Silence reigned in the room over the next five minutes as she stroked him, kissed him, licked him, and nipped him; laughing softly as she enjoyed herself thoroughly.

Just when he thought he might burst into an orgasm, she stopped the torture to move away and remove her own shorts. Kicking the garment out of the way, she jumped on him, her legs wrapped around his waist, and grinned wildly when he thrust into her wet centre, his hands splayed over her bottom. He settled her over the edge of the table he had been working on as he pumped into her, climaxing quickly as he couldn't stop himself.

She came right at that moment, her teeth sinking into his shoulder, her whole body trembling in the aftermath. When she was finally able to draw breath, she asked, "Did you enjoy the massage?" her lips brushing his ear.

"The best ever," he declared, kissing her forehead. "You know something, babe?" he asked as an afterthought, "It's only because of you that I'm looking forward to this trip."

"Sweetheart!" She kissed his cheek, brushing a soothing hand over his head. "You need to loosen up."

He sighed. "Believe me, you help me loosen up, all the time. Do you think I'm falling in love with you?" he asked, an expression of wonder on his face.

Dipika's heart thundered against her rib cage as she gave him a wary glance. She did not want to read more than what was actually there. "You think so?" she asked in a soft whisper.

He pressed his lips to the top of her head, hugging her close to his chest, feeling a sense of deep calm settling over him. A calm he had not felt since the time he had got to know of his trip to Surat. "I think I am, babe."

She hugged him back, burying her face in his chest even as a huge sigh shuddered through her being.

It was the morning of Bhoomi's engagement when Chandulal was walking up and down the veranda, eagerly waiting for Mudit to turn up. He had been sure that the boy would have arrived by now, wondering what must have delayed him.

Right at that moment, Mudit was having a shower in his suite at the Surat Marriott Hotel which was a ten-minute car ride from his parents' home.

They had arrived at the hotel only at around seven the earlier evening and checked into the suite which Mudit had booked until the time they planned to leave on the next Monday.

"Like it?" he asked, standing behind her with his hands on her shoulders as Dipika gazed at the bedroom and the sitting room.

"It's lovely, Mudit. It must be costing you a bomb. I hope you're going to let me share…" She was effectively silenced by Mudit who captured her mouth in a deep kiss.

Letting go of her mouth when they came up for much-needed air, he looked into her eyes. "You came on this trip as my guest. I'm not going to let you spend any money, okay?" His voice was firm, brooking no arguments.

"Okay, host," she responded cheekily before lifting her face for another kiss.

It had been late when they went to bed and later, spent a lazy morning making love.

"Are you sure you don't want to come with me now?" he asked, giving her a hopeful glance as he shrugged into a white half shirt, before tugging on a pair of jeans over his long legs.

Watching him avidly as he covered up his wonderful body, she gave him a firm nod. "Yes. This morning is for your parents, Mudit. Go and meet them by yourself. Time enough for me to meet your family in the evening."

"I'm going to miss you," he said, tucking his shirt tails into the waistband of his jeans, meeting her gaze through the mirror.

She blew him a kiss. "Absence makes the heart grow fonder," she said, giving him a wink.

"Bullshit!" he growled, turning suddenly to grab her naked body into his arms. "I have a good mind to take off my clothes and…"

"Mudit!" She pressed her hands on his chest to stop him from doing anything like that. "You are late. Go!"

"Okay, I will let you miss me," he grumbled before thrusting his feet into a pair of slip-on shoes.

"I promise," she said, giggling at him. "Bye," she called out, pressing the tips of her fingers to her mouth and blowing him a kiss as he left the suite.

Mudit reached his parents' house barely fifteen minutes later and was not really surprised to see his father pacing the veranda at the front. With a soft sigh, he parked the car and got out to go meet him.

"Mudit!" Chandulal took his son's hands in both of his and smiled up at him.

"Pappa!" Mudit freed his hands to bend down and touch his father's feet.

"You've come, Mudit." Sharda's voice was a screech as she rushed out to greet her eldest born.

"Yes, Mamma." He touched her feet too before hugging her. Somehow, he felt lighter meeting his mother and father, wondering if it had something to do with the fact that he had found the love of his life. More than that, he was confident that Dipika loved him, even if she had not told him about her feelings in so many words.

"You are late and you must be tired after driving all the way from Mumbai. Did you leave very early?" His mother chattered all the way as they stepped into the hall.

Mudit glanced at the hall, feeling a sense of nostalgia hit him. This was the first time he was entering his family home in the twenty years since he had gone to live with his grandfather. The room appeared smaller somehow; maybe because he had grown up so much from the twelve-year-old who had viewed it the last time.

When he felt a tug on his arm, he turned around to glance at his mother. "You were saying, Mamma?"

She laughed softly, looking up into his face, love gushing from her heart. "I said you must be feeling tired, driving all the way from Mumbai."

He gave a shake of his head. "No, Mamma. I'm not tired." Time enough to mention that he had arrived the earlier evening; that too, only if necessary.

"Did you have time for breakfast? Otherwise, there is both *dhokla* and *khandvi*, your favourite snacks."

Mudit's eyes lit up at the thought of food. He loved food at any time of the day. It was a good thing that he lived an active life and did not tend to put on weight. "I would love that. Do you have fried *mirchi* to go with it?" he asked eagerly.

Sharda laughed, clapping her hands. A typical mother, she was so looking forward to feeding her son who had been absent from her life for two decades. "Of course, *beta*. I'll bring everything right now."

Chandulal gave a sigh of relief when his wife left to go to the kitchen. Or he had been worried of not getting a word in between. "Why don't you bring your luggage inside?" he suggested, turning to look up at his strapping son, proud of the way he had turned out.

Mudit took a deep breath before answering. "There's no luggage, Pappa."

"What?" Chandulal's voice was loud as he gave his son a shocked glance. "Are you returning to Mumbai after the engagement? I told you there's another programme on Tuesday, then on Thursday, Saturday and the wedding is on Sunday. Do you plan to keep travelling back and forth?"

"Um... er... Pappa, I..." He cleared his throat before speaking firmly, "I'm staying until the wedding, Pappa. It's just that I've booked into a hotel..."

"Sharda, Sharda, come here right now." Chandulal shouted at the top of his voice. So much so that the three servants who worked for the Trivedis came rushing into the hall to find out if they were needed. Arvind and Dinesh, who had been smoking on the terrace secretly, came rushing down two floors to reach the hall in record time. Bhoomi, who had been trying on some new make-up, threw the lipstick on the dressing table to come running down the stairs. Everyone stood gaping at Chandulal wondering what had set him off as it was obvious that he was in a roaring temper.

Sharda, who was the only one who was aware that her husband's bark was worse than his bite, came walking at her own pace, carrying a tray loaded with the snacks she had promised her son. "What happened, *Mudit na Pappa*? Why are you shouting?" she asked coolly, handing the tray to Mudit.

Arvind met Dinesh's gaze, both of them grimacing when they saw their older brother standing next to their father. They neither could help the trace of envy when they noticed how handsome Mudit was, and turned out so fashionably too. He was tall, way taller than either of them, taking after their mother's genes. Oh, why did he have to come? They had all been living so peacefully before his arrival.

Bhoomi took a hesitant step forward, her gaze on her oldest brother. She had been three years old when Mudit had gone to live in Mumbai. She barely knew him, except for what she had heard from her mother. "Mudit *Bhai*..." she called out, taking another step forward.

"Bhoomi?" Mudit turned to the young woman who was walking towards him, taking hesitant steps. Feeling an unexpected and powerful gush of emotion as he recalled her as a baby, he swiftly walked to her before gathering her in his arms in a fierce hug. It was not her fault that he had been packed away to live with his grandfather. Moving a couple of inches away, he looked down at her affectionately. She was as tall as their mother, and well built; and so young and beautiful. "Are you happy with this marriage?" The question popped out of his mouth even before he could gather his thoughts together.

"Yes, *Bhai*." She gave him a shy smile through the tears which filmed over her eyes, the same grey shade as his.

"I'm glad. I can't wait to meet your Roopak Kandoi this evening."

Bhoomi blushed delightfully before burying her face in her brother's shoulder. "I'm also glad you are here, *Bhai*. It has been such a long time."

Mudit sighed. "I know." But he was not going to apologise for his absence from her life. After all, it was not his fault.

Chandulal stood there in the centre of the hall, glaring at Mudit who was conversing with his sister. Unable to keep quiet any longer, he turned to his wife and shouted as if she was deaf. "Do you know that Mudit is staying at a hotel?"

Sharda turned pale as she lifted her stricken gaze to her husband before transferring it to Mudit. Just a moment ago, she had been so happy when she saw the way he had greeted Bhoomi, with so much affection. And then this! "Mudit?" Her voice was a tortured whisper as she sought to verify if what her husband had told her was the truth.

"*Ji*, Mamma." He walked over to where his mother was standing, his arm around Bhoomi's shoulders as he pulled her along with him. He had not only noticed his brothers standing near the staircase, but also the hostile expression on their faces. Time enough to greet them later.

"Is your Pappa telling the truth?" Sharda asked in a pathetic voice.

"What is Pappa saying?" he asked, playing for time.

"You heard him," she said, her grey gaze accusing. "Are you really staying at a hotel?"

"Mmm, yes, Mamma," he replied firmly, looking directly at her.

"But... but how could you do that? We..." She stopped speaking when Dinesh laughed in triumph.

Both the younger brothers came forward to join the rest of the family in the middle of the room. Helping himself to a piece of *dhokla*, Dinesh said, "Does this mean I can have the corner room?"

Sharda slapped her third son's hand when he would have taken another piece of *dhokla*. "Why don't you let Mudit eat? He's hungry," she said, giving him an angry glance, her gaze imploring him not to speak any further about the room which had been prepared especially for Mudit.

"So am I," insisted Dinesh, sneaking a hand to take one more piece.

"I would like to have something too," said Arvind. Turning to his oldest brother, he said, "Why don't you have something, Mudit? Or she won't let us eat anything." Barely three years younger to him, Arvind had been the closest to Mudit when they were children.

Picking a piece of *khandvi*, Mudit suddenly recalled that it was Arvind's most favourite snack. Turning towards him, he offered it to his younger brother, shaken by the powerful feelings which enveloped him. "Here you go, Arvind," he said, feeding his brother.

Arvind recalled the time when the two of them used to sneak into the kitchen on hot, summer afternoons, to taste the many snacks Sharda had prepared against orders she had taken from neighbours. Catching his older brother's eye even as he munched on the *khandvi*, Arvind gave Mudit a broad smile.

"Arvind." Mudit let go of Bhoomi to hug the man who was not only his brother, but his partner-in-crime. "How are you, bro?"

"I'm happier now that you are here," said Arvind, his voice shaky with emotion. There had been many a night when he had cried after Mudit left to go to Mumbai. He had received many beatings from his father when he repeatedly nagged Chandulal about Mudit's return, not receiving a reply regarding the same. "I've missed you, Mudit."

A deep sigh shuddered through Mudit's being before he let go of Arvind to turn towards his other brother. "Dinesh?" He opened his arms invitingly.

Dinesh shook his head, his gaze wary. He felt a tad betrayed by Arvind's behaviour. Had they not agreed, only yesterday, to keep Mudit at arms' length? What was Arvind doing now, hugging the enemy and eating from his hand? "I don't remember you," he declared rudely.

Mudit's arms fell to his sides, a disappointed look on his face. But he was not going to blame Dinesh. Maybe he had felt cheated by his oldest brother, the same way Mudit had felt betrayed by his parents. Eight days was a long enough time to do repairs. Giving a shrug, he sat down on a chair to help himself to the snacks his mother had provided.

Sharda went to sit next to Mudit. "Are you really going to stay in a hotel?" she asked him in a pathetic voice.

"Yes, Mamma. I think it's for the best." Mudit answered firmly.

"But... but, this is your home," she protested, turning to her husband for support.

"Exactly," said Chandulal briefly, not knowing quite how to deal with the situation. After all, Mudit was not like the other two boys, whom he had managed to shut up only the other day. His eldest born had been a veritable stranger for all of two decades.

Mudit shook his head. "No, Mamma. This is not my home. It stopped being my home when you sent me away to live with grandfather. I can't imagine living here now." Turning to Dinesh, he said, "You should take that room, Dinesh. I'm not going to be staying there."

When Dinesh crowed in delight, silent tears poured down Sharda's cheeks before she buried her face against Mudit's shoulder.

Mudit reached out to hug his mother, letting her cry. While he could see her view point, he had no intention of changing his mind. Why would she want him home suddenly, after letting go of him when he had been a child? If she could accept the situation then, she definitely could do it now that he was a fully grown man. A typical Gemini, he was ready to give them his affection, but he needed his personal space.

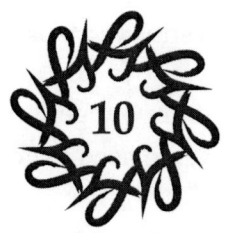

10

Mudit returned to the hotel room only after five, to see Dipika relaxing on a chair, her feet on a footstool, reading a book.

"Hey! How did it go?" She left the book on the table to go up to him, throwing her arms around his waist to hug him close.

Hugging her right back, he kissed the top of her head. "All good, better than I thought actually."

She looked into his happy face, grinning at him. "I'm so glad."

"I'm sorry I left you all alone until now. I…"

She placed a hand over his mouth, stopping him from speaking further. "Don't you dare apologise. I had a relaxing day anyway."

"Miss me?" he asked, kissing one corner of her mouth.

"Always. So, what happened?" She wanted to know everything as she had been a tad anxious about his broken relationship with his family members. She could see that it affected him badly.

"My parents wanted me to stay at home, but I told them it was no go. I could connect with Bhoomi and Arvind. In fact, it was almost like we picked off from where we left off twenty years back. But Dinesh isn't so forgiving."

"That must be your younger brother."

"Yes. By the way, we need to get back by 6.30. Can you get ready soon?"

"Of course," she said, going on her tiptoes to give him a kiss on his mouth. "Can you manage to do that?" she teased.

"Hahaha. I'm going to take a nap, if you don't mind. I…"

"Of course not. You go ahead. I'm off to take a shower."

"Unless you want me to join you?" he asked, an eyebrow up in query even as his eyes lit up with desire.

She shook her head. "We'll never be ready on time. You go have your forty winks and I'll get ready. I'll wake you up in a while."

He kissed her before letting her go. Removing his shirt and pants, he fell on the bed and went to sleep almost immediately.

Dipika smiled at her sleeping lover before going inside the bathroom. She took a leisurely shower, washing her hair and blow drying it, letting it fall into natural curls over her shoulders and back. She stepped out to open the wardrobe and pulled out the sari she planned to wear. It was a plain silk sari in a rich shade of ivory with a wide sapphire blue border on both sides and a matching *pallu* in the same shade of blue. While the sari was plain, the blue silk blouse with short sleeves and a narrow back was heavily embroidered in cream and gold, held together with two buttons at the back. Once she wore her blouse and petticoat, she walked over to the bed and shook Mudit's shoulder. "Wake up, Mudit, it's time to get ready."

He came wide awake immediately, smiling when he saw her leaning over him. "Give me a kiss," he invited, opening his arms wide.

She moved away, shaking her head. "You'd better get out of the bed before we kiss."

"Stubborn woman," he grumbled, following her instruction and walking over to her. "See what you do to me," he said, taking her hand and placing it over his tumescent manhood.

She squeezed him gently with her hand as she lifted her face for his kiss which turned out to be more heated than she had expected. Pulling away, she said, "I think a cold shower will help."

"You can't be so cruel," he said, pretending to be shocked.

"It's almost six."

"Shit!" He rushed towards the bathroom with her laughter ringing in his ears, a soft smile breaking out on his face. He felt such a sense of lightness, the kind he had never felt in a long time.

"You look awesome," he said, when they both were fully ready. He could not take his eyes off her sari-clad figure, seeing her in the traditional wear for the first time. "I like you in a sari."

With pink colour washing over her beautifully made-up face, she reached over to kiss his freshly shaven cheek. "You look amazing yourself. So much so that I can't wait to return to the room," she responded in a throaty whisper.

He tilted his head back to study her blushing face with half-closed eyes. "And what do you plan to do once we get back? Study my amazing looks?"

"Minus your *churidhar-kurta*, and your boxers, yes."

"Ouch!" he grimaced when his body responded painfully to her softly worded promise. "I asked for it, I suppose."

"You did," she grinned, tucking her hand into his arm as they stepped out of their suite. "I hope your family wouldn't mind you thrusting me in their midst," she said, a tad anxious about their reaction. After all, they were keen to arrange his marriage with someone else.

"Are you worried?" he asked, turning the car out of the gates to the compound, surprised to hear the trace of anxiety in her voice. Dipika was confident, in all circumstances. He was sure of it.

"Not worried, but a little bothered, definitely. Especially with you mending fences with them only recently... I don't want to throw a spanner in the works."

He reached over to take her hand in his, pressing it briefly before returning his own hand to the steering wheel. "You could never do that, babe. You are my girlfriend and people had better accept that if they want me to accept them."

She blushed fierily when she heard the possessive note in his voice, feeling touched as she leaned her head on his shoulder.

They reached Mudit's family home a couple of minutes later, Dipika's eyes going wide as she looked at the sprawling, three-storied structure. It looked beautiful and regal at the same time. He parked the car at the far-right side of the compound before escorting Dipika into his home.

The scene which met them now was way different from what Mudit had experienced in the morning. The hall was beautifully decorated with garlands of marigolds and fairy lights, while thick carpets were spread in the centre for people to sit. The sofas and chairs had all been pushed towards the walls, for people who preferred to sit on them. There were two beautifully decked low wooden chairs placed at the furthest end, meant for the couple who were getting engaged.

Mudit was glad that the decorators, who had arrived at around noon, had finished with their work and were on the verge of leaving.

"Oh, hello. Glad you are here. Now you can take care of any early arrivals while I go get ready," called out Arvind, when he saw his older brother step inside the hall.

"Oh good. But wait, I would like you meet someone."

Arvind stepped forward eagerly, his gaze lighting up when he noticed the beautiful woman on Mudit's arm.

"This is Dipika Sanyal, my girlfriend. And Dipika, this is my brother, Arvind."

"Hello Arvind." Dipika smiled at him, offering her hand for a shake.

Taking her hand in his and shaking it, Arvind gave her a winning smile. "Hello, Dipika, welcome to our home."

"Thank you," she said sweetly.

"You go on now and get ready. Where are the others?"

"They should be down in five, I think. I shooed them away some time back."

"Good. And the caterers?" asked Mudit, now that he knew all about the arrangements.

"Oh yes, they are out in the north side of the garden, setting up their stalls. Why don't you go and check them out?"

"Maybe I'll wait until Pappa or Dinesh come down."

Arvind gave a nod, turning towards the staircase. "Makes sense. I'll see you soon." He suddenly stopped in his tracks. "I'm sorry, but Dipika, would you like some tea?"

"You should go, Arvind. Or you'll be late. I'll take care of Dippy here."

"Dippy, huh?" Arvind gave his brother a naughty grin and a wave before disappearing up the stairs.

Mudit laughed softly, an affectionate expression on his face. "We used to be so close, you know."

"I can't see anything different now," she said, pressing his hand, happy for him.

Sharda came rushing down the stairs. "Oh, there you are Mudit. There's a problem. What's the time?"

"Is that the problem?" asked Mudit, smiling at his mother. "It's fifteen minutes to seven."

"Oh God! People should begin to arrive now. But this girl… oh God, what am I going to do?" She twisted her hands in a frenzy as she came down to stand beside her eldest born. It was only then she noticed the lovely young woman standing beside him.

"Mamma, this is Dipika, my partner. And Dipika, this is my mother, Sharda Trivedi."

"*Namaste*, Aunty," said Dipika, bringing her palms together in a greeting as she smiled at Mudit's mother who was as tall as she was.

"Partner means?" asked Sharda, wondering about the relationship between the two.

"Later, Mamma. You were worried about something…?" he prodded her.

The surprise on her face vanished to be replaced by worry. "Bhoomi isn't ready yet. Her beautician has messed everything up. She now hates her hairstyle and dislikes the make-up even more. Where will we get someone at such short notice? I don't know if she will be ready on time. And Bhoomi will simply refuse to leave her room unless she feels she looks fine. I don't…"

Mudit gave his mother a dazed glance, having never come across such a problem before in his life. Office emergencies, he could deal with. Staff unrest, most definitely. But beautician problems… he turned his helpless gaze towards Dipika, wondering if she could think of an answer to Bhoomi's problems.

"I can help, Aunty. Where's Bhoomi's room? Show me the way."

"Do you know how to…?" Sharda stopped when Mudit laughed. "What?" she asked him with a frown.

"There's nothing about beauty that Dipika does not know of," said Mudit proudly. "She runs a modelling agency." When Sharda gaped at him uncomprehendingly, he said, "Which is Bhoomi's room? Let me take Dipika to her."

"The second room on the right. But…"

"You wait here for me, Mamma. Just in case someone comes. I'll be with you once I introduce Bhoomi and Dipika."

The two of them raced up the stairs. "Do you think you can have her ready in half an hour?"

"Don't you worry about all that," said Dipika, giving him a smile. "I'm used to working swiftly under pressure. Let me deal with this."

Mudit knocked on the door. A lady of about forty years opened the door to glare at him. "Who are you?"

"Is Bhoomi here?" asked Mudit, refusing to be cowed down by the woman's animosity.

Before she could respond, Bhoomi called from inside, "Mudit *Bhai*, is it you? Come on in." Seeing her brother, she fell into his arms, wailing. "Oh Mudit! I don't know what to do. I think I'm going to look horrible for my own engagement. I…"

"Shh," he shushed her, a hand stroking her head. "Nothing like that is going to happen. Dipika here is going to make you look gorgeous in a jiffy."

Moving away from him, she asked, "Who's Dipika?"

He stared aghast at his young sister's face. It was full of bright and unnatural colour, her cheeks a brilliant pink, while her eyelids were covered in blue paint. "What the hell? Why is your face painted?" he asked, shocked at the way she looked; at least twenty years older than she actually was. And so… so unnatural was the word which came to his mind.

Bhoomi wailed some more. "I told you I'm going to look terrible. I..."

"No, no." He shook his head firmly. "This is Dipika. She's my friend and partner. Dipika, this is my little sis Bhoomi."

"Hello, Bhoomi. Please sit down at the dressing table." She took a cotton ball lying on a tray and soaked it with some body lotion lying on the table. Turning to Bhoomi, she quickly ran the damp cotton over her face and neck, both the front and the back. She had to repeat this three times before the thick layers of make-up finally came away. "Can you please wash your face quickly and come back here? Do you have a gentle face wash?" She asked the younger woman who was rushing towards the bathroom. When Bhoomi nodded, she said, "Wash your face twice, once with warm water and then again with cold water. Oh, and your throat as well." Turning to the other woman and presuming she must be the failed beautician, she requested, "Can you get me some ice cubes?"

"Why should I? And who the hell are you? Do you know who I am? Let me tell you. Ushma Shah is the name. And I have been running a successful beauty parlour for the last fourteen years. I..."

Dipika turned away to look at Mudit. "Can you organise for some ice cubes?"

"Consider it done," he said, going out of the room.

Bhoomi stepped out of her attached bathroom after having washed her face, staring at Dipika in fascination. She could not help thinking that Mudit's friend looked lovely; well dressed and beautifully made up. She felt a surge of confidence that this stranger might be the person to help her right now. But will she be able to get her ready quickly?

"Sit down, Bhoomi. What do you plan to wear?" asked Dipika, checking the array of make-up on the dressing table.

"Bhoomi, what you are doing is not right. How can you allow a stranger to dress you up? And this woman looks nothing like a beautician. You are taking a major risk…"

Bhoomi turned in a flash to glare at the older woman. "Can you please leave? We can talk all about it tomorrow."

"How dare you?" Ushma took a couple of steps towards Bhoomi, only to be stopped in her tracks when she felt a heavy hand on her arm.

"I think you had better leave," said Mudit, his stance threatening as he glared at the frowning woman. He handed over an ice bucket to Dipika, without taking his eyes off the beautician.

Ushma turned away and left the room, carrying her make-up case along with her. Let them manage without all the material required to transform Bhoomi.

"Do you need any other help?" asked Mudit, looking at Dipika who was busy sorting through the available make-up items.

"I don't think so. Just make sure we aren't disturbed. We are in a rush here."

"Sure. See you soon." He left.

Bhoomi pointed to the silk *gaghra choli* spread out on the bed, in a lovely shade of turquoise, heavily embroidered with silver thread and sequins. "That's what I'll be wearing."

"Jewellery? Wait, I'll go check. In the meanwhile, here, hold this over both your eyes." Dipika handed her two ice cubes wrapped up in tissues. She walked over to the bed to open the jewellery box and smiled when she saw the heavy earrings, necklace, and bangles of old silver, set with turquoise—a perfect match for the clothes. Bhoomi had excellent taste, it seemed. "These are delightful, Bhoomi."

Bhoomi smiled on hearing the compliment. "Thank you. I must say that you look so pretty. If I can look half as lovely after you finish dressing me up, I'll be so grateful." Her eyes were shut as she continued to hold the ice cubes over them.

"Thanks. But you already look so beautiful, your skin so flawless. I plan to use light make-up as I don't want to take away from that. Will you be okay with that?"

"I'm so glad you think so. This is exactly what I was arguing with Ushma about. She was using heavy make-up and I simply hated it." She met Dipika's gaze via the mirror and smiled at her. "Thank you so much for helping me out at such short notice."

"Wait until I'm through. I only hope you like it." Dipika removed a small case which she usually carried with her in her handbag. It contained make-up brushes, eye make-up and the like. She removed the ice pack from Bhoomi's face before setting to work.

To begin with, she unpinned the elaborate hairstyle which Ushma had created so painstakingly. Careful not to hurt her, Dipika worked quickly at removing the pins before brushing Bhoomi's silky hair which fell to her waist in a thick curtain. Using the curling iron on the dressing table, she brushed her hair into a massive tumble of curls before gathering it up in a knot. "How tall is your fiancé?" she asked suddenly, pausing in her task.

"Eh?" Bhoomi, who had been watching the transformation in fascination, met Dipika's gaze via the mirror. Turning pink, she said, "Way taller than I am."

"Good. I had to make sure before creating a top knot." Bhoomi was already tall, at five feet eight inches in her bare feet. Dipika quickly made a simple knot, leaving a few curls loose at the sides of her face. "Do you like it?"

Bhoomi, who had never done anything but either plait her hair or leave it loose, was thrilled to bits at her new hairstyle. "I love it. I hope you will teach me how to do it," she responded with a shy smile.

"Definitely." Dipika smiled right back at the younger woman before quickly applying light foundation to her face. She finished it all with a touch of peach eye shadow, turquoise blue eyeliner, and peach gloss for her pouting lips. Her cheeks carried a tinge of peach, just a tad of highlight.

Bhoomi stared at her face in the mirror, her eyes glowing with excitement. This is exactly how she had visualised herself, exotic without overdoing it. Clapping her hands, she jumped to her feet. "Thank you so much."

Dipika gave her a quick hug even as she drew her towards the bed. "You will need to hurry."

"Yes." Bhoomi quickly removed her nightie and drew her *gaghra* over her head before fitting it into place at her waist.

Just as she was wearing her blouse, Dipika asked, "Your footwear?"

"Under the dressing table," came Bhoomi's muffled voice as she pulled her *choli* into place.

Carrying the shoe box over to where Bhoomi was standing, Dipika went behind her to help her with the three pairs of strings at the back of her blouse, tying them into intricate bows. She then draped the matching net *dupatta* embellished with rhinestones which shimmered every time she moved. "Would you like me to pin it to your shoulder? Or do you want to leave it loose?" asked Dipika.

"Pin it, please. Here." Bhoomi handed a semi-precious brooch to Dipika before removing the necklace from the jewellery box.

Dipika helped her with the jewellery and finally the young lady was ready. They both smiled at each other when there was a knock on the door at precisely that moment. "Bhoomi, are you ready?" asked Dinesh. "Mamma wants you to come down right now."

"Yes, I am," said Bhoomi, throwing the door open with a wide smile on her face. "What do you think?" she asked her brother.

Dinesh whistled under his breath. "Incredible. I wouldn't have believed it if someone had told me yesterday that you were beautiful. But looking at you now…" He burst out laughing when she punched him with a fist. Catching hold of her hands before she could hit him again, Dinesh hugged her. "You look amazing, sister."

"I'll let you live," she said, smiling at him. "Oh, did you get a chance to meet Dipika? She's the one who helped me with everything." Turning to Dipika, she said, "This is Dinesh, my brother."

"Hello Dinesh," said Dipika, smiling at the young man who resembled Mudit the most.

"Hello beautiful. Lovely meeting you," greeted Dinesh, floored by the stranger's beauty. "I can't believe that we have never met before." He shook his head in a half daze.

Locking her arm in his, Bhoomi laughed as they all moved towards the staircase. "That's because Dipika isn't from Surat. At least, I don't think so." Turning to her right, she asked, "You are also from Mumbai, right?"

"That's right. I live not all that far from Mudit's bungalow," said Dipika, keen to make it clear to Dinesh that she was with Mudit.

Dinesh's face darkened with disappointment on hearing her words. Damn! His oldest brother seemed to have it all! And he felt a strong streak of jealousy rush through him. "What can I offer you to move to Surat?" he asked Dipika, giving her a flirtatious smile.

Dipika smiled right back at him as she slowly shook her head. "No force is going to drag me away from Mumbai. I run a successful business there which thrives on my presence."

"You run a business? How cool is that!" Bhoomi was totally impressed with Mudit's friend. "We need to talk, please."

"Any time. But let's get this show on the road first," said Dipika, eyeing the couple of hundred guests who had arrived by now.

"You have worked magic," said Mudit in Dipika's ear, giving her a winning smile. Turning to Bhoomi, he said, "You look stunning, my dear sis."

Bhoomi laughed softly, thrilled by the compliment. "Your Dipika is the best."

Dinesh stood to one side, glaring at the three of them.

11

Mudit sat on the carpet to one side of his sister and her fiancé, Dipika right beside him. He never let go of her hand throughout the ceremony; not when the *panditji* read out the wedding contract, not when the couple exchanged garlands, not when relatives and friends walked up to congratulate the couple.

Dipika was only too happy to sit next to him, her hand held in his as she looked at the glowing Bhoomi and the handsome Roopak who was so obviously in love with her. As for Mudit's parents, they sat next to Mudit, closest to the couple. There had been no time for proper introductions and she realised that it did not really matter.

After the ceremony was over, everyone got up at once, their chatter adding to the festive atmosphere in the hall.

While Mudit's father Chandulal had been an only child, his mother Sharda had two brothers and two sisters, living in Surat. They had all of them come along with their spouses, children, and grandchildren. Each one of them was eager to get reacquainted with Mudit, taking his hand and speaking to him emotionally. It was a while before Arvind and Dinesh could persuade the guests to move towards the garden where the dinner buffet had been arranged.

Finding his parents standing by themselves, Mudit drew Dipika over to them. "Mamma, Pappa, this is Dipika Sanyal. She's my best friend." Turning to Dipika, he said, "You met my mother. This is my father, Chandulal Trivedi."

Dipika brought her palms together in a traditional greeting. "*Namaste*, Uncle, Aunty."

"You are a Punjabi." It was not a query but a declaration by Chandulal, his forehead pleating in a small frown.

"Yes, Uncle."

"Are you both partners in business?" asked Sharda, wondering about their relationship. She could not deny that the girl was not just beautiful, but really nice too. The way she had helped with Bhoomi's emergency had truly impressed Sharda.

"No, Mamma, we are not." Mudit did not bother to explain further. Well, he really could not tell her that Dipika was literally his sleeping partner, could he? And he still was not a hundred per cent sure if he wanted her as his life partner.

Sharda bit her lower lip, not knowing what to say as she could not still understand why he called her his partner in that case. He had also mentioned that she was his best friend. Did that mean Dipika was Mudit's girlfriend? Sharada was confused. "I am yet to thank you, Dipika. It was very sweet of you to help with Bhoomi's make-up. I really don't know what would have happened if you had not offered to do it. And I must say she appears stunning after whatever you did to her."

Dipika laughed softly. "It was my pleasure, Aunty. Bhoomi is naturally beautiful, just like her mother," she said.

Sharda was floored by the compliment, a broad smile on her face as she patted Dipika's shoulder. The girl had such great manners too, she thought to herself.

Dipika had noticed that Mudit and Bhoomi got their height from their mother's genes. Sharda was the same height as Dipika, at five feet, nine inches tall. While Mudit's father was barely an inch taller than his wife. Both Arvind and Dinesh had taken after their father and were not as tall as Mudit, who was at least two inches taller than six feet.

Chandulal's gaze zeroed in on Dipika's left hand tucked into her son's right hand. Were they in love or something? Then what about Suchita? The girl's parents had approached him for Mudit's hand. She was also Roopak Kandoi's cousin. Chandulal was not keen on any bad feelings with the groom's family. How to make his son understand that?

What Chandulal was not aware was that Mudit was making a statement by holding Dipika's hand, refusing to let it go even for a moment. Mudit did not want anyone to be under the mistaken impression that he was available on the marriage market.

"I need to talk to you, Mudit."

"Of course, Pappa. Tell me."

"In private," said Chandulal, pinning his son with his gaze.

Dipika pulled her hand from his hold, her gaze imploring him to speak to his father, alone.

Not at all liking it, Mudit let go of her with great reluctance to walk with his father a few steps away.

"Where do you live in Mumbai? Who are all there in your family? And what do you do?" Sharda was full of questions as she wanted to know everything about the woman who had accompanied her son all the way from Mumbai. She began to believe that there must be something going on between the two of them.

"I live in Vile Parle. I…"

"Isn't that where Mudit lives?" asked Sharda.

Dipika smiled. "That's right, Aunty."

"Are you both neighbours? Have you known each other long?"

Dipika had to work hard to stop herself from laughing at the way Mudit's mother was shooting questions at her, without allowing her to finish telling her about herself. Shaking her head, she said, "We aren't neighbours. My bungalow is about twenty minutes away from his home. And I have known him for three months or so."

"Oh!" How to find out if they were an item? Maybe she should set Bhoomi to ferret out the information. "And your family?"

"I have an older brother. I live with him and his family."

"What about your parents? Do they live in Punjab?"

Dipika shook her head from side to side. "Our family has lived in Mumbai for four generations. My parents are no more, Aunty." Her voice was soft as she uttered the last few words.

"Oh, my dear! I'm so sorry to hear that." Sharda threw an arm around Dipika's waist. "You must be missing them terribly."

Dipika's mouth drooped at the corners. "Yes, Aunty, I do. Though it has been thirteen years after they died in a freak accident. It was my brother who took care of me after that."

"My poor child." Sharda hugged Dipika close before kissing her on her forehead. "I must say that your brother has done an excellent job though," she said, smiling at the younger woman. She might not be a Gujarati girl, but she would make Mudit a wonderful wife is what the mother had concluded by now.

"Thank you, Aunty," smiled Dipika, her eyes gone bright with the sheen of tears. "I'll let Krish know. I'm sure he will be thrilled to hear that."

"Is he married? Your brother? You mentioned his family."

"Yes, Aunty. He's married to Sanjana and their son Kabir is seventeen months old." She opened her phone to show their pictures to Sharda, sure that the older woman would like that.

Sharda oohed and aahed at the beautiful family for a few minutes. Giving her phone back, she said, "I wonder what they are talking about for so long? We can't leave all the guests in the boys' care." Raising her voice, she called out, *"Mudit na Pappa!"*

Turning in their direction, *"Aavu chu,"* he responded, walking towards his wife.

Mudit stood exactly where his father had left him, a heavy scowl on his face.

Dipika quickly walked over to him before taking his hand in hers. "Is everything alright?"

"Never is," he growled, his gaze still on his father who was walking towards the garden along with his mother. Taking a deep breath, he turned his gaze to Dipika. "You remember I told you about the suitable girl they had planned for me?"

"Hmm... mmm."

"I believe she is Roopak's cousin. And my father isn't keen to upset the groom's family."

Her eyes went wide in disbelief. "So, what does he expect you to do?"

"Exactly what I asked him." Mudit rubbed his free hand over his eyes. "Family!" he fumed. "By what right does he think he can choose my life partner? He dumped me when I was barely twelve."

Uncaring about the guests who were returning to the hall in groups after finishing dinner, Dipika threw her arm around Mudit's waist, hugging him close. Taking a few deep breaths, somehow hoping he would calm down, she spoke softly, "Today is your sister's big day. Please don't lose your cool."

A deep sigh broke forth from the depth of his being. "You're right, Dippy. Let's go." He gently removed her arm from around his waist and took her hand firmly in his before guiding her towards the dinner buffet.

They mingled with the guests, Mudit introducing her as his friend, before walking over to where Bhoomi and Roopak were sitting at one of the circular tables arranged all over the garden which was brilliantly lit with halogen lamps placed at strategic intervals.

"Would you like me to get you anything?" asked Mudit, seeing their empty plates.

Roopak turned up to look at his oldest brother-in-law-to-be and smiled. "Nothing for me, thanks. I'm stuffed. But I'm sure Bhoomi would love to have some *gulab jamoon*."

"Not me, no," groaned Bhoomi, rolling her eyes at her fiancé. "I've eaten enough for two, with everyone wanting to serve us something or the other."

Roopak laughed. "She's right. We don't need anything, bro. Why don't you get your dinner?" He then turned to look at Dipika enquiringly.

"Oh, by the way, this is my friend and partner, Dipika Sanyal. And Dipika, this is Roopak Kandoi, Bhoomi's fiancé."

Once they greeted each other, Bhoomi spoke, "It is thanks to Dipika that I was ready on time. And looking halfway decent too. I…"

"Halfway decent?" Roopak gave her a heated glance. "You look gorgeous," he insisted.

Mudit laughed, leaving his blushing sister alone with her fiancé as he drew Dipika towards the buffet spread.

It was almost midnight when a silent Mudit drove back to the hotel. Dipika sat next to him, not uttering a word as she realised that he was still preoccupied with his father's lecture. He had told her all about it, in bits and pieces, in between chatting with his horde of relatives who clamoured for his attention. And of course, they had all been curious to know about the woman at his side.

Thank God that his father had stopped with introducing Mudit to only Roopak's parents. Time enough to meet the rest of the people from the groom's side as Mudit was fully occupied connecting with his own people. There had even been a number of neighbours who remembered him as a child and craved his attention. After all, he was one of their own who had made a big name for himself in Mumbai. They were all dying to know why he had never returned to his hometown, not once during the last twenty years. But they were too polite to ask about it.

Dipika smiled when she realised that her boyfriend—okay, partner, if that is how he wanted it—was extremely popular. Imagine that! He had been a preteen when he left home; and was returning after two decades. But still everyone was keen to get reacquainted with him. She leaned her head on his shoulder with a happy sigh.

"Tired?" asked Mudit, as they entered the gates to Surat Marriott Hotel.

"A bit."

Handing the car key over to a valet, Mudit guided her towards the bank of elevators, his arm around her waist. They quickly undressed before falling on the bed, too tired to do much else but to go to sleep.

But it was only Dipika who was fast asleep once her head touched her pillow. Not Mudit! He was wide awake as he recalled his conversation with his father, unable to let go of his resentment...

"Who is this girl? This Dipika Sanyal. What does she mean to you?" were the opening words Chandulal greeted his son with, the moment they stepped away from the two women.

Mudit's first instinct was to tell his father to mind his own business. Losing his cool, he said curtly, "I don't really owe you an explanation, Pappa."

The colour left Chandulal's face when he heard his son's rude words. "Mudit…"

Realising that he had hurt his father, Mudit took a deep breath before saying, "You will have to excuse me. I didn't mean to be rude, but I am not used to answering to anyone, you understand? Even when *Bade Pappa* was alive, I used to lead a free life; come and go as I pleased." He paused as a deep sigh shuddered through him. "If you must know, Dipika and I share a live-in relationship. I…"

"Do you plan to marry her?" asked Chandulal, continuing in his own line of thinking despite Mudit's explanation earlier.

Mudit grimaced. "I am not sure at this point, Pappa."

"What about her? Doesn't she expect you to make an honest woman of her?"

Mudit laughed, unable to stop himself. "She is an honest woman whether we marry each other or not. She is honest enough to accept herself for exactly what she is." As he spoke, he realised it was the truth. And he found his admiration for Dipika increasing tenfold.

"And what is she?"

"A successful career woman," said Mudit, proudly.

"But that isn't enough, is it? What about family? Children?"

Mudit's imagination kicked in as he saw Dipika working on her laptop with a couple of children running all around her. After all, the first time he met her, she had been with her nephew. And it was obvious that little Kabir adored his aunt. Suddenly, Mudit realised that he wanted to be the father of the imaginary children playing around Dipika. But what in case they did not end up marrying? What if she married some other man? He was startled to feel a deep pain in the region of his chest. What the fuck! He turned his dazed face towards his father. "I don't know, Pappa. It's her life. It is for her to decide."

Nooooo! He was only lying to himself. He very much wanted to be a part of Dipika's life, be alongside her when she made life altering decisions, such as marriage, children, and whatever.

Chandulal shook his head. "In that case, you should seriously consider Suchita Kandoi. She is a beautiful woman and will make you an ideal wife. Not one of these modern women who are more interested in their careers than having a family. Suchita will keep you grounded and will give you as many children as you want. Do you understand? Let me set up a meeting the day after tomorrow, before the *Sangeet* ceremony begins." He looked up at his son's face, trying to read his reaction. "Is that alright with you?" he added as an afterthought when he noticed the deep frown on Mudit's face.

"Give me some time to think, Pappa. I'll tell you tomorrow." While he wanted to refuse outright, he realised that it was not going to make a difference with his father, who would only continue to persist. He had to come up with an alternate plan. He breathed a sigh of relief when his mother called out to his father before Chandulal could say anything more on the subject.

And after that, he had made sure that he did not spend a moment alone with his father.

Mudit gave a huge sigh as he came to the present, turning to look at the peacefully sleeping Dipika next to him. He silently got out of the bed and went to the sitting room, not keen to disturb her. Pouring himself a shot of brandy, he stepped out into the balcony, leaning on the railing to stare out at the vast sky.

It was not what his father had said that had disturbed him. After all, no one could force him to marry this Suchita woman, not if he did not want to. Which he most definitely did not; no offence to her. But it was the scene from his imagination—of Dipika sometime in the future, with children of her own. And he realised that he did not want her to bear another man's child, children, whatever. In fact, he could not abide the thought of her with another man. If Dipika wanted to marry and settle down, have children, it was going to be with only one man. And that man was Mudit!

He tilted back his head to swallow the brandy and smiled slowly when it burned down his throat, finally clear about the direction he wanted to go in.

When his best friend Kiara fell in love with Arjun; and Arjun, also his best friend, fell head over heels for her, Mudit had been happy for them. But he could never understand this 'love' thingy; the need to have a single partner throughout the whole span of one's life. Not until today. More than the feeling that he would not be able to live the rest of his life without Dipika, what struck him strongly was the fact that he could not stomach it if Dipika spent the rest of her life with some other man.

Talk about twisted logic!

All he had to do now was wait until they returned to Mumbai. After that, he was going to woo Dipika Sanyal, until she agreed to become his wife, his life partner. It looked like his subconscious mind already knew what he wanted; which was the reason why he had introduced Dipika as his partner to all the members of his family, instead of as justremoving a friend.

He continued to lean on the railing and stare at the sky, suddenly enamoured by the stars shining down at him. How beautiful they appeared! And they so reminded him of Dipika's twinkling eyes laughing up at him.

Yes, he had fallen in love with her, well and truly. His heart rejoiced when he finally admitted the feeling to himself. Now all he had to do was make her fall in love with him. But then, the passionate Gemini was completely confident of achieving it. With a smile and a wave to the twinkling stars, he turned to go back inside the suite, walking into the bedroom to lie next to the love of his life.

She came half-awake when she felt his arm around her waist as he spooned his body close to her back. "Not sleeping?" she queried, in a soft voice.

"Just going to," he said, pressing his mouth to her bare shoulder. "Go back to sleep." And they both fell into a dreamless sleep.

Mudit's phone rang the next morning when they were serving themselves from the breakfast buffet at the hotel. Seeing Bhoomi's face on his phone screen, he smiled as he took the call. "Hey, good morning, bride."

"Mudit *Bhai*! Good morning. Where are you?"

"At my hotel. We are just going to have breakfast."

"But I thought you both will come over here for breakfast," wailed Bhoomi, thoroughly disappointed.

"Well, it's like this, Bhoomi. Pappa is chasing me to meet some woman he would like me to marry. I'm unable to convince him that I am not interested. I…"

"Of course, you are not. You are interested in Dipika."

"And how do you know that?" asked her brother in a startled voice.

"Come on, Mudit *Bhai*. You take me for a fool or what? The way you two look at each other, it is obvious to anyone with a pair of eyes that you belong together."

Oh my God! Was it true? If that were the case, why had he not realised it before last night? And what about Dipika? Was she aware of it? He was terrified of meeting her glowing brown gaze as he sat down next to her at their table.

"Mudit *Bhai*, I actually called to talk to Dipika. But I don't have her number."

"Dipika is right here. I'll give my phone to her. And will also send you her number," said Mudit, handing his cell phone to Dipika, mouthing, "Bhoomi."

"Hello Bhoomi, how are you today?" asked Dipika, a smile in her voice. She really liked Mudit's young sister who was so affectionate.

"Good morning, Dipika. I was fine until a few minutes ago when Mudit told me you guys aren't coming over today. Now I am miffed," she said.

Dipika laughed softly. "Don't be. Your wedding is in barely a week and you need to keep your cheer up."

"But I want to spend as much time as possible with you people. And I called to actually ask you about the other ceremonies. I don't know if I can impose on you to do my make-up. So, if you can help me find someone…"

"Listen, Bhoomi," interrupted Dipika, "It's not an imposition at all. I enjoyed doing what I did last evening. And with more time for planning and prep, I think we can do even better. I'm here for your wedding and I would love to be of help."

"Yaaay!" Bhoomi pumped her fist in the air as she made a noise which was close to a war cry, making Sharda jump at the breakfast table. "Sorry, Mamma," she said before turning her attention back to Dipika. "Thank you, Dipika. That's really so nice of you."

"Tell you what? Why don't I take you make-up shopping? And maybe some more accessories which you might require? You take pictures of all the outfits you plan to wear. What if I pick you up in a couple of hours? Works?"

"Do you mean it?" Bhoomi couldn't believe her ears, her voice shivering with excitement. She had a number of friends, and was really close to a few of them too. But none of them had any fashion sense. While Dipika was so damn cool.

"Of course, I do." She turned to give Mudit an apologetic glance. "Do you mind?" she asked him, closing her hand over the phone's mouthpiece.

He gave her a wide grin, shrugging. "Only if you want me to tag along with you."

"Hahaha!" Dipika burst out laughing before removing her hand and speaking to Bhoomi. "Two hours from now. What say?"

"Yes, yes and yes."

"See you," said Dipika before handing over the phone to Mudit.

"Hey, it looks like you girls have a plan," said Mudit into the phone.

"Yes, Mudit *Bhai*," responded Bhoomi enthusiastically. "Do you want to come with us?" she added as an afterthought.

Mudit shuddered. "No, thank you. Unless you are dying for my company?" he asked cheekily, closing one eye as he looked at Dipika.

"Hehe! Not while shopping, no," said Bhoomi firmly before saying bye.

"Hey, thanks," said Mudit, pressing his lips to Dipika's cheek, "That was really sweet of you."

"Sweet, my ass. You don't really believe that, do you? I'm only doing it because I really like Bhoomi and I love shopping." The truth was that she felt touched by his words and was astonished by the feeling of shyness which suddenly enveloped her.

"Whatever!" he said, forking a piece of omelette and offering it to her. "Why don't you take the car with you?" he offered.

"Are you sure? You don't need to go anywhere?"

"Mmm..." he stretched lazily, drawing her gaze to his toned midriff when his t-shirt separated from his cotton shorts, "I was thinking of getting my hair cut and maybe a facial. What do you think?"

"I think it's a great idea. Your mug needs straightening up, anyway." Her eyes twinkled with laughter before she ran away from him.

"Just wait until I get my hands on you!" he said mock threateningly, signing the bill quickly before rushing after her towards the elevator.

"I can't wait," she said in a whisper, her eyes clinging to his.

"Do you think we have time for a quickie before you leave?"

"Why do you think I offered to pick Bhoomi up after another couple of hours?" she countered, wiggling her eyebrows at him as they entered the empty lift.

"I always knew you were smart," he said, leaning down to take her mouth in a smouldering kiss, his hands squeezing her bottom even as he pressed her close to his lower body.

He carried her out of the elevator, holding her slender body close to his chest as she fumbled with the door before pushing it wide open. Kicking it shut with his foot, he went all the way into the bedroom before letting her slide down his body to stand in front of him next to the bed.

Her gaze clinging to his, Dipika pushed his t-shirt away from the waistband of his shorts to caress his flat midriff with eager hands. "Can you remove this for me?" she asked in a hoarse voice, not taking her gaze off his.

"Gladly," he growled, reaching down to lift the t-shirt and pull it over his massive torso and right above his head.

They had been together for three months, but Dipika could not help but be amazed every time she set eyes on his well-muscled and toned body. Reaching up, she pressed her mouth to his throat before kissing her way down his body until she reached his navel, before going on her knees. Unaware of the mewling noises coming out of her throat, she stroked his navel with the tip of her tongue, relishing his taste. Tucking her thumbs into the elastic waistband of his shorts, she pulled it down his muscular thighs, smiling mischievously when she saw that he had gone commando.

"I like the way you dress," she said throatily, curling a hand around his rigid shaft.

Mudit, who had been watching her avidly from behind half-shut eyes, groaned when he felt the scrape of her nails against his manhood. Gripping her head with one hand, his fingers digging into her thick hair, he pushed her head towards his arousal.

Lifting her face to meet his hot and needy gaze, she drew her damp tongue down his length, smiling again when she heard him groan louder than before. She took him in her mouth when she reached the tip and sucked on him greedily.

Mudit felt his body move of its own volition as his penis thrust into her mouth, his need turning rapacious with every stroke of her tongue.

Her left hand running down one thick and strong thigh caressingly, Dipika sucked on him some more, her right hand holding him firmly in place.

"Dippy…" He pulled himself out of her mouth to lift her up and lay her down on the bed. Pressing his mouth to hers in a deep kiss, he ripped her dress down the front, the need to touch her heated skin driving him crazy.

Running her hands down his back, she smiled at the play of muscles before gulping suddenly when she felt his mouth against her breast; having removed her bra with a single twitch of his fingers. "I love it when you do that, you know?"

He smiled against her breast. "Mmm…" He suckled her sensitive nipples in turn, reaching down with a finger to touch her core, smiling some more when he found her all wet and ready, for him. Turning on his back, he pulled her above him, pulling her legs on both his sides.

Realising his intention, she impaled herself on his stiff cock, gasping when he slid inside her vagina to fit into the sheath so perfectly. She began to ride him slowly and then fast, egged on by his hands at her breasts, squeezing them even as he stroked the distended tips with his thumbs.

He watched her, his Dippy, as she rode him, her head thrown back, her hair falling down her back like a river of dark silk, her pale breasts filling his eager hands to perfection. And he gasped when he felt her come, a soft scream ensuing from her throat, pushing him towards his own orgasm as she continued to ride over him.

Dipika flopped over Mudit's chest, totally spent, grateful for his strong arms as they gathered her close. It was a very long time before either of them could breathe normally once again.

A little more than an hour later, Dipika pressed the tips of her fingers to her mouth before placing them on the sleeping Mudit's cheek, a soft and adoring smile on her face. She knew that he had not slept until at least 2 am last night and was glad to notice the relaxed expression on his face.

"See you later, my love," she said in a whisper before leaving their suite, shutting the door quietly behind her, leaving the 'do not disturb' sign turned on outside the door.

Bhoomi was jumping about in excitement when Dipika entered the hall of the Trivedis' home.

"Hello, I see that you are ready." Dipika greeted Mudit's sister with a smile.

"Yes, I can't wait to go," said Bhoomi, taking Dipika's hand in hers and dragging her inside. "But before we leave, Mamma and Pappa want to meet you."

Wondering what this could be about, Dipika went along with Bhoomi, into the area further beyond the hall, which was used as a sitting-cum-dining room. Chandulal and Sharda were seated on a sofa, watching TV.

"Come, my dear," called Sharda the moment she saw Dipika enter the room.

Chandulal put the TV on mute before turning to look at Mudit's partner, unable to deny that the young lady was truly beautiful, just as Sharda had pointed out to him earlier when they had spoken about her. "And she is well mannered too. See the way she stepped in to Bhoomi's rescue. And you know something, Dipika is a successful business woman in her own right."

"How would you know that?" Chandulal had asked grumpily.

"Mudit told me when I asked him. I am sure she earns a lot of money, almost as much as Mudit does."

"Huh!" Chandulal had refused to be impressed. But somehow, his wife had argued and argued until she had convinced her husband that Dipika might make their eldest born a wonderful match. At least, Sharda was sure that her husband was convinced with her argument.

Just now, Sharda got up to take Dipika's hands in her own before seating her next to her on the sofa. "Bhoomi said you were taking her shopping today."

"That's right, Aunty. We thought of getting everything she will require for all the four functions which have been planned."

"That's a good idea. So, you will be getting her ready for all the functions?" asked Sharda, truly touched by the younger woman's offer.

"Yes, Aunty. I am looking forward to it," said Dipika, with a smile.

"That's so nice of you, Dipika. Uncle said he didn't have an opportunity to speak with you yesterday.

He..." Sharda turned to frown at her silent husband, indicating that he should say something.

Chandulal, who had been watching the way his wife was carrying on, was damn irritated. First Mudit, then Bhoomi, and now Sharda—what kind of black magic was this Dipika woman weaving over all of them? He was still stuck with the idea of marrying his son off to Suchita, who was truly a *sanskari chhokri* as against the modern Dipika, who was also a Punjabi into the bargain. The father was not at all keen about the idea of his offspring marrying a woman who not only ran her own business, but who must also be a meat eater. Such a daughter-in-law would never suit his family, he believed. He had comfortably forgotten the fact that his own son had not been with the family over the last two whole decades.

Removing the scowl from his face with great effort, he gave Dipika a grim smile which did not reach his eyes. "So, have you known Mudit for long?"

Dipika wondered where this was going. Had Mudit's mother not asked her a lot of questions yesterday? "About three months, Uncle," she responded politely. She knew it for a fact that Mudit's father did not like her. But then, what did it matter? She was not really looking for a 'popular woman of the year' award; definitely not from Mudit's estranged family.

"And do you plan to marry him?" asked Chandulal outright.

Dipika shrugged, meeting the old man's piercing gaze head on. "It's too early in the day, Uncle. We have not thought that far."

"What does your family have to say about you travelling alone with him like this? Staying at a hotel together?" It was rude, even for Chandulal.

"My life is my own, Uncle. My brother does not interfere in it."

He gave a sharp nod. "I don't understand this modern generation. No family, no culture, no tradition," he muttered, totally vexed. It was not that he was not aware about the changing trend in the younger generation, but that did not mean he approved of the same.

"The only culture and tradition I know is to let people be; allow them to follow their own path and dreams; to help if and when I can; and to spread happiness," said Dipika, softly but firmly. She was not going to lie down and take his lecture for whatever reason. So what if he was Mudit's father? Chandulal had no right to run her life.

Bhoomi, who had just placed a tea tray on the centre table, brought her hands together, clapping hard. "I like what you say, and agree with you completely." And she was so glad that Roopak lived by the same maxim too.

Chandulal did not like the way Dipika stood up to him, and found the woman damn rude. How dare she speak to an elder like this? Disagreeing so openly? Mudit was an idiot to want to marry this girl. Actually, Chandulal was not even sure if his son wanted to marry her. He was just annoyed that Mudit had brought Dipika over to his home town and let her mingle with his family and friends. What were they going to think of Chandulal and Sharda for allowing this?

It was a good thing that Suchita had not come for the engagement yesterday; all because her best friend had got married on the same day. Phew! But the girl will be coming for all the other functions.

How was Chandulal going to face Suchita's parents or even Roopak's parents for that matter? Roopak's father and Suchita's father were brothers; and both were keen on taking Mudit as their son-in-law. Thinking quickly, he came to a conclusion. Lifting his furious gaze to Bhoomi, he glared at her, giving a small shake of his head, indicating that she should leave the room. He also tilted his chin slightly towards Sharda, continuing to stare at Bhoomi, making sure his daughter understood that she was also to take her mother along with her. He wanted to speak to Dipika alone, damn it!

Her face darkening with foreboding, Bhoomi turned towards her mother helplessly. Her father was capable of bringing the roof down if she did not follow his orders, and instantaneously too. "Mamma, can you come with me for a minute? I need your help with some of the outfits we bought." She took her mother's hand in hers and dragged her out of the sitting room, into the hall, and up the staircase.

Dipika stared at the tea tray uncomprehendingly. What had happened just now? Why did Bhoomi drag her mother away from the room, leaving her alone with Mudit's father? She was not comfortable with Chandulal as she could feel the heat of his disapproval flowing towards her in waves; his frown so dark.

"Listen, Dipika Sanyal!" It was an order rather than a request when Chandulal spoke to her in a stern voice.

Dipika lifted her gaze from the tea tray and looked at the older man, meeting his gaze unflinchingly, waiting for him to say what he was obviously dying to tell her.

"Mudit is from a traditional Gujarati family and we have been settled in Surat over five generations. Fortunately, or unfortunately, he went to live with his grandfather in Mumbai and got estranged from all of us. But that does not mean that he has stopped belonging to the Trivedi family. I understand you youngsters have loose morals and don't think twice before going to bed together. But all that is fine for a man, you understand? But not for a woman. I don't know what kind of an upbringing you have had, but then I don't know what kind of culture a Punjabi family follows. Maybe it is accepted in your family if you sleep around, but not in ours, no. Let me be upfront with you. We have a suitable girl from a nice family, especially chosen for Mudit."

He took a long and shuddering breath after that intense speech, his piercing dark gaze fixed on the young woman who was sitting in front of him, not batting an eyelid. There was no expression on her face at all as she sat straight, staring right back at him, fearlessly meeting his flinty gaze. Which only managed to anger Chandulal all the more!

"Your being here when the meeting happens between Mudit and Suchita is the most inconvenient thing, you understand? I want you to not attend any of the functions for Bhoomi's wedding from here on. It is best that you leave Mudit alone with his family." He raised a supercilious pepper and salt eyebrow at her, as if to ask her if she understood his message correctly. "Ideally, you should leave Surat immediately."

Was he not asking her a lot? But then, it was Chandulal Trivedi's house and his daughter's wedding. The man was footing the bill for everything, damn it! He definitely had a say as to who could attend the wedding and who couldn't. Dipika got up from the sofa slowly, feeling a kind of numbness taking hold of her. In all her twenty-nine years, she had never come across anyone who did not want her around. It was a strange feeling and one she found difficult to swallow, let alone digest.

But she had to leave, now! She definitely did not want to be in a place where she was not welcome. That she was here on Mudit's invitation did not matter. After all, he himself had no sense of belonging with the Trivedi family. As for Mudit's father, he could not have made it clearer that she was unwelcome in his home. Taking a deep breath, she turned to her right and began to walk towards the entrance of the house, her mind working furiously.

For one thing, she did not want to leave Bhoomi in the lurch. The young woman did not deserve it. Breathing deeply, Dipika tried her best to wipe away the expression of shock on her face, though unable to do much about her pallor, as the colour had completely receded from her countenance. She walked outside the front door before sending Bhoomi a WhatsApp message requesting her to come out to the car.

While she waited for her, she thought about how to handle the situation without upsetting Mudit. If she mentioned anything at all, with the kind of relationship he shared with his father, chances were high that he would up and leave for Mumbai along with her, turning his back completely on his family. And Dipika could never be the cause of it. No way! She had to come up with an idea, and quickly too; a reason why she had to be back in Mumbai or any Timbucktoo for that matter.

She knew how hurt Mudit was by the way his parents had packed him off to live with his grandfather in Mumbai when he was only a child. He had felt abandoned by his own family. Now, he was back home for the first time in twenty years. And Dipika did not want to be the one to spoil his homecoming.

Bhoomi came rushing towards the car and knocked on the window. "Hey, did you have tea at all?" she asked when Dipika wound the window down.

"I didn't want any, not after the heavy breakfast I had," said Dipika. "Do you have all the pictures? Get in and let's go."

Bhoomi got inside and pulled the seat-belt across her slim body. Just as Dipika drove out of the gates, she said, "You forgot to say bye to Mamma." She spoke in a soft voice which had a question in it. "Is everything alright, Dipika? Did Pappa say something to you?" There was an anxious note in the younger woman's voice.

Dipika pressed the brake swiftly as the car careened out of control. Stopping under a tree in the quiet lane, she turned to glance at Bhoomi with an expression of resignation on her face. She would not mind making a clean breast of it. After all, she was fuming so hard that she was all set to burst. And why not talk to Bhoomi who knew her father only too well? And frankly, Dipika did not really care if

Chandulal's daughter got to know that he was worse than what she probably believed him to be. It was only Mudit whom Dipika wanted to protect. "Listen Bhoomi. If I tell you something, will you promise not to share it with Mudit?" She lifted her palm face up, waiting for the younger woman to make the promise.

The colour receded from Bhoomi's face when she saw the stony expression on Dipika's. "What happened, Dipika?" she asked again.

"I need your promise first, or I can't talk about it."

"I promise." Having no choice, Bhoomi agreed reluctantly. There was a time when she used to hate her parents for sending Mudit *Bhai* away from home. Oh yes, at three years and five months, Bhoomi had not been so young that she had not felt the absence of her oldest brother. Only, for a long time to come, she had believed that he was going to return. But he had not, not until yesterday, which was twenty years too late; when she was on the threshold of going to live in her husband's home. She could not help the sneaky feeling that her father was once again doing something to Mudit's life. Something her brother was definitely not going to like. Or why would Dipika ask for her promise not to divulge anything to Mudit?

"Your father is keen for Mudit to marry someone called Suchita. He feels that my presence here will throw a spanner in the works. He…"

"Did Pappa tell you to leave?" Bhoomi was shocked, unable to believe her ears. She knew her father was a strict person, but telling a guest to go away was too much, even for him.

Dipika gave a small nod. "See Bhoomi, I don't exactly blame your father. He's old school and wants his son to marry a traditional woman."

"Mudit *Bhai* will never listen," insisted Bhoomi, taking Dipika's hand in hers. "It is you he loves."

Dipika gave her a wan smile. "Well, I don't really know about that." She gave a sigh before plunging in. "I think you have probably understood by now that Mudit and I are lovers. But that is it. We don't have any other kind of commitment. So!" She shrugged, unable to stop her lips from drooping at the corners. Not for a moment did she believe that Mudit will quietly agree to marrying this Suchita. That was not the point. She was simply unable to digest the fact that she was unwelcome in his family home; deeply disturbed that his father had told her so to her face. It hurt like hell!

Bhoomi did not know quite what to say. Yes, she had guessed that the two of them must be lovers as they were staying in a hotel on their own. But that still did not mean that Mudit did not love Dipika. As for Dipika, it was obvious that she adored Bhoomi's brother. "I'm sorry, Dipika, I really am," she said, a tear falling down her left cheek.

"Oh Bhoomi, don't! Please don't cry. This time is so special for you and you should be happy. Roopak is a great guy and I'm sure you both will have a wonderful life."

Bhoomi smiled through her tears. "I totally agree about that. He's nothing like Pappa, who is such a strict disciplinarian. I'm actually planning to study further, you know. Which I couldn't do here because Pappa was dead set against it."

It was Dipika's turn to remain silent, as she really had nothing to say in response to Bhoomi's statement. Drawing a deep breath, she gunned the engine, saying, "Let me do something. Earlier, I had got in touch with the Lakme showroom in Sargam Shopping Centre; taking an appointment with them for your sake. We will go now and choose all the make-up you need. Better yet, let us hire an expert who will dress you up on all the days."

Bhoomi placed a hand on Dipika's arm. "You have decided to leave?" she asked in a small voice.

"I don't really have a choice here, Bhoomi. Your father is hosting the wedding. I can't come if he says I can't. You do understand that, don't you?" Dipika suddenly felt a powerful urge to be back in Mumbai, in familiar surroundings, amidst her family and friends. She wanted to see Krish and Sanjana, speak to them if only to confirm that she was a normal human being. That was how badly Chandulal's despicable treatment had shaken her.

With great difficulty, Dipika kicked up enough enthusiasm to help Bhoomi choose everything she required. She also sat down with the younger woman and Rashi, a beauty consultant working for the high-end brand and between the three of them, they made an elaborate plan of what was to be done regarding hairstyle and make-up for the bride-to-be. Once it was all settled, they had lunch at Wok on Fire, a Chinese restaurant in the same mall. Originally, the plan had been to take Bhoomi back to the hotel and have lunch with Mudit. But Dipika was not sure if she could handle both the brother and the sister at the same time. She did not want to make a mistake by divulging the truth to him. She had sent him a message earlier to tell him that they had been delayed and would not be able to get to the hotel in time for lunch.

And now, finally, finally, it was all over. Dipika stopped the car outside the gates to the Trivedis' home. "I don't think it would be a problem for you to manage all this stuff, do you?" she asked Bhoomi. After all, there were only two large shopping bags and they were not all that heavy.

Bhoomi gave her new friend a sad look. "You are not going to come in to say bye to Mamma?" she asked pathetically.

"It is best that I don't, Bhoomi," said Dipika firmly. She never planned to cross this threshold, ever in this lifetime. She was still too shaken that someone disliked her so much that he did not want her in his home.

Bhoomi removed her seat belt to reach across and give Dipika an awkward hug. "I am going to miss you, terribly. And so will Mudit *Bhai*, I am sure."

Dipika shrugged. Well, it was not her fault, was it? She only wished she had told Chandulal off to his face. She should not have left without uttering a thing. How dare he insult her so horribly? A typical Libra, all the words she could have said, came to her mind only after she had walked away. Especially now, after she had completed the task she had set for herself, to help Bhoomi.

"I wish you luck, Bhoomi. Have a great wedding." Dipika could barely smile through her raging emotions, as she looked at the younger woman's pinched face. "And enjoy yourself."

"I hope we can stay in touch." Bhoomi walked around to speak to Dipika through the window.

"Why not? You have my number and I have yours."

"Are you leaving today itself?" Bhoomi felt a powerful sense of betrayal steal over her. She had made such a good friend, who was already lost to her, all because of her father.

"Yes, bye." Dipika gunned the engine and drove away speedily. Or she knew it for a fact that Bhoomi would stand there talking for as long as she could. After all, the young lady had made it obvious that she did not want her new friend to leave.

She drove around for a bit until she came across a garden. Sneh Rashmi Botanical Garden, read the large name board outside. She parked the car outside before purchasing a ticket and walked in. Luckily, it was not too hot for a late afternoon as she walked along the tracks laid out, not really noticing the flowering plants or the towering trees, her mind working furiously. She needed a convincing excuse to return to Mumbai today itself. Or Mudit was capable of breaking down all her arguments.

A family emergency?

No, that would never work. For all she knew, he might insist on accompanying her back to ensure that everything was back in control before returning to Surat in time for the next ceremony. And her lie would simply fall apart.

Office work! An unexpected meeting lined up with a foreign brand who was in India, insisting on speaking to the head of Amber Modelling Agency and none other. Dipika stopped in her tracks suddenly to snap her fingers, startling a couple of magpies which had been chattering in the nearby bush. They both complained vociferously before taking off, making her laugh softly; as she finally felt lighter. She turned around quickly to walk towards the entrance. Time to go back and tell Mudit that she needed to get back to Mumbai. She ran the upcoming conversation in her mind a few times before she had the answers to all probable questions he might come up with.

"Hey!" Mudit shut the book he was reading to get up and walk to the door when it opened to admit the woman he had fallen in love with. She was as beautiful as always, clad in a pair of stretch jeans which made her legs appear longer than ever; teamed with a sexy sleeveless top of printed cotton in cheerful shades of red and orange. Throwing his arms around her, he kissed her long and hard. "I missed you."

She pouted up at him as she studied his newly trimmed hair which still fell down to touch the nape of his neck. As for his face, it was clean shaven and looked handsomer than ever after the facial he must have got done. "You look beautiful," she said in a stage whisper, her eyes laughing up at him. She was still coming to terms with the metrosexual man he was.

"I'll take that as a compliment, thanks," he said, giving her a wink. "Do you want coffee?"

"Yes, please," she said, going forward to plonk down on the double sofa.

He quickly poured the pre-mixed coffee he had ordered barely minutes ago into two mugs and brought it over. Handing one mug to her, he sat down next to her on the sofa, sticking close to her slim body. "You look sexy in this outfit," he whispered into her ear.

"I do?" She fluttered her eyelashes at him playfully as she turned to look into his heated grey gaze.

"Totally. So, what are we going to do this evening? We can stay here if you're too tired to go out. Or we…"

Keeping the half-full coffee mug down on a side table, Dipika turned to speak to him earnestly. "Listen, Mudit. Something has come up."

"You sound serious," he said, wondering what was going on.

She sighed. "Yes, it is, kind of. Because it's good as well as not so good."

He shook his head slowly. "That just made everything as clear as mud. Why don't you enlighten me?"

"A major clothes brand from Europe is looking for a foothold in India. This is the first time they are venturing outside the European continent. Their CEO is here and is insisting on meeting with the head of Amber."

He grimaced. "Which is you."

"Exactly. I'm so, so sorry, sweetheart. I didn't…"

He pulled her into his arms and hugged her close to his chest. "Do you think you'll be done before the wedding on Sunday? You can take a flight back here."

Dipika could not believe she had heard right. Had he accepted her words at face value? It all appeared too easy suddenly. "You don't mind?" she asked, lifting her startled gaze to his.

"Of course, I do, totally. But then, I understand how important this meeting must be to you. Or you wouldn't be leaving me like this, in the lurch. And you are such a professional too. I can relate to your work ethics, Dippy. I'm actually proud of you." Time enough to speak about his love for her after they were back home in Mumbai. "So, when do you think you will be done?" he asked.

No, she refused to feel guilty, just because Mudit believed that she would never leave him in a lurch, unless it was an emergency. Well, was this not an emergency? Being thrown out of the Trivedis' home by the head of the family himself? Dipika shook her head in response to his question. "I don't really know. This is not going to get done with just one meeting, you realise?" She continued when he nodded. "The first one is scheduled for tomorrow morning."

"Ouch! Does that mean you have to leave today itself?" he asked; "I'll take you back," he added.

Dipika pressed a hand over his chest, stroking it over his steadily beating heart. "No, Mudit. Your family needs you; and you need them too, even if you refuse to accept it. I will take a cab."

"Are you sure?" he asked, his forehead pleating in a small scowl. He knew and accepted her for the independent woman she was. It was just that he did not want to let her go. He could easily get back into a relationship of sorts with his people only because Dipika had been with him at his side. Even yesterday morning, when he had gone home all by himself, he had drawn strength from the fact that she was not too far away. She had helped in keeping him grounded when he had needed it the most. He was going to miss her, terribly. But he did not tell her the words. She needed to go and he did not want to stop her in any way.

"Yes, Mudit. Give me a kiss," she said, lifting her face to him.

He obliged, kissing her deeply as if there was no tomorrow. They were going to be apart for the first time for more than twenty-four hours after that chance first meeting at the *dandiya* grounds.

Framing his face with her hands, Dipika looked deeply into his eyes. "I'm going to miss you, sweetheart. I'm going to throw myself so deeply into my work, that it's going to be Monday before I have time to breathe."

He smiled on hearing her words. "I have no such escape. I'll be thinking of you all my waking hours and dreaming about you while asleep." He leaned down to kiss her some more.

"It's almost five. I'd better leave. Oh, by the way, I've set up a proper beautician for Bhoomi. And she has everything she requires. Give her a hug from me, will you?"

"I'll do that," he said, getting up. "Do you need my help with your packing?"

"That would be great, thanks."

They quickly packed her suitcases before Dipika called for an outstation cab. It arrived after fifteen minutes and she left, just like that.

Dipika leaned back in her seat, shutting her eyes closed, unable to believe that she had got away so easily.

As for Mudit, he sat down in the sitting room, staring up at the ceiling morosely, missing her already as one would a limb. Taking out his phone, he called Arvind's number. "Do you want to come over for a drink?"

"At your hotel?" asked Arvind, thrilled at the idea of clubbing at a five-star hotel.

"Yep. Do you think Dinesh will tag along?"

"I'll ask him."

"You do that. Shall I expect you at seven?"

"You bet."

13

"Hey, are you having fun?" Dipika was thrilled to hear from Mudit on Sunday morning. She had pretended to be extremely busy through the week since her return and had kept sending him messages on and off, discouraging him from calling her.

"I'm breathing freely now, if you want to call it fun."

"I don't understand. What…?"

"Do you have a busy day today?" he asked.

"Not really."

"Why don't you come home in fifteen?"

"Mudit! Where are you?"

"I should be reaching home by that time."

"You mean in Mumbai?" She could not believe her ears. Today was Bhoomi's wedding day. What the hell was he doing here in Mumbai? "But why are you not in Surat? Bhoomi's wedding is today, isn't it?"

"It isn't. You come over and we'll talk, okay? I have to take this other call." He disconnected the phone when he saw Kiara's face on the screen.

Dipika shook her head in a daze. What must have happened for Mudit to not attend his sister's—dear

Bhoomi's—wedding? She left the garden room where she had been having coffee and went to her room to have a shower before pulling on the first pair of shorts and t-shirt she could get her hands on; stepping into her running shoes and rushing out of the house. Meeting Sanjana on her way, she called out, "I'm out for the day."

Sanjana smiled and waved, noticing the happiness on her sister-in-law's face for the first time since she had arrived home on Monday, close to midnight. It was only a couple of days later when Dipika had told her the reason why she had come rushing home from her holiday with Mudit even before it had really begun.

"Mudit's father had the gall to tell you to get lost?" asked Sanjana, her eyes gone wide with shock. How dare he? "You should have told Mudit something, I feel."

Dipika shook her head even before Sanjana had finished speaking. "No, Sanju. There is already a wide rift in their relationship…"

"Why am I not surprised? His father is obviously a control freak. I can understand why Mudit will not be a party to it." Both Krish and Sanjana thought really high of Mudit Trivedi. They did not say much only because no one knew if the relationship was going to be permanent or not. Neither of them was keen to push Dipika into something she was still not sure about, like marriage, which was a major commitment to both partners involved.

Dipika smiled. "That's it in a nutshell. Mudit's father wants to control him, totally unaware that it's never going to happen. But I definitely didn't want to remain there as an unwanted guest. And it was not the right time to tell Mudit the truth; not when their relationship was still so fragile."

Sanjana had hugged her sister-in-law and best friend, not having an answer to that. And now, it looked like Mudit was back home and Dipika was rushing over to meet him. But wait! Wasn't the wedding planned for today? How could he have returned this morning? Sanjana was thoroughly baffled. But she had no one to ask about it as Dipika had already gunned her car away, out of the compound.

Dipika reached Mudit's house a few minutes before he did. Ringing the bell, she gave Kishorilal a wide smile. "How are you, Kishore Uncle?" she greeted him.

"I'm fine, child. Mudit is on his way and should be reaching at any moment."

"Yes, Uncle," she said, grinning joyously. She could not wait to be in his arms.

"Let me arrange for some coffee."

"And maybe some snacks for Mudit. I'm sure he must be hungry." If she was not mistaken, he must have left very early in the morning as it was not even ten o' clock yet.

Kishorilal gave her a nod, smiling as he went towards the kitchen. He knew that Mudit was always hungry. And maybe will require a wholesome breakfast instead of a couple of snacks. Which was the reason why he had ordered the cook to make *poori* and spicy *aloo ki sabzi*, just the way the boy liked it.

Dipika turned when she heard a car drive into the compound. Unable to stop herself, she stepped outside the door, a welcoming smile on her face when she saw Mudit getting out of the driver's seat. "Mudit!" she called out.

"Dippy!" He walked over swiftly to gather her into his arms. "I love you!"

"What????" Her head fell back in surprise when she looked up into his handsome face. Handsome, but drawn.

"You heard me," he said, suddenly losing his confidence. What in case she threw it right back in his face, after the way his father had treated her? But then, was she not here to meet him? He had only to ask and she was here; even throwing herself into his arms. He stared down into her lovely face, and did not miss the lurking sadness at the very back of her eyes. "I'm sorry, Dippy," he said suddenly. "I'm sorry for the way my father spoke to you. The bastard! I wish you had told me immediately. I would have torn him apart with my bare hands." He drew her inside the house to push her down into a sofa before sitting next to her. "Kishore Uncle, I'm home," he called out to his Man Friday.

"I... I don't understand. How did you know?" asked Dipika, her voice a confused whisper. But she could not stop the feeling of joy spreading in her chest when she heard the anger in his voice, on her behalf. "Bhoomi gave me her promise."

"Well, she couldn't stop herself, not under the circumstances."

"What circumstances?" Dipika did not understand.

"Well, we were four against one. With Arvind, Dinesh and Mamma on my side, we finally dug the truth out of her. But then, I think she was only too relieved to have it off her chest."

"But wait. She's getting married today, in a couple of hours. What are you doing here?" Dipika glared at him. After all the efforts she had gone to, to keep the truth from him, how could he ditch his family, especially his sister, like this?

Mudit gave her a maniacal grin. "The wedding is cancelled."

"WHAT???" Dipika jumped to her feet, almost knocking the tray from Kishorilal's hands, just as he was bending down to place it on the low table in front of the sofa. She turned around to steady the old man, worried that he might topple to the ground. "I'm so sorry, Uncle. I didn't see you."

"Obviously not," he muttered, turning to look at Mudit. "Welcome home, Mudit."

"Thank you, Uncle. It's good to be home," said Mudit, turning right back to Dipika.

Understanding only too well when his presence was not required, Kishorilal left the two of them alone.

"Well, it's a long, long story. Why don't you sit down and have some breakfast? I'm famished. Come." He reached over to pull her down on the sofa next to him before eating his way through hot *pooris* soaked in ghee, relishing the delicious *aloo sabzi* which accompanied them.

Dipika shook her head in amazement as she watched him eat. She could not imagine swallowing even a tiny piece of *poori*, however tempting it was. Pouring a mug of coffee, she sipped from it as she continued to watch him, a feeling of adoration warming her heart. Had he said 'I love you' to her? Except there were too many things yet to be explained and she could not quite absorb his words of love.

"Aren't you going to have any?" asked Mudit, looking up from his plate and giving her a lopsided smile.

She shook her head. "Nope."

"In that case, you can have me for breakfast," he offered, winking at her.

Hot colour rushed up her face as she met his heated glance. "I would love that. But you might want to digest your food first."

"What? No way am I going to wait that long."

"Well then, what are we waiting for?" she asked, getting to her feet.

He rolled his eyes mischievously. "Some women are tempted by five-star dinners. Others by jewellery. Some, by branded clothes. But all Dippy wants is…"

"Hot, steamy sex," she growled, taking a fistful of his shirt to pull him to his feet, "now."

"Anything for you, babe," he said. "Will you let me have some coffee though? I promise not to linger over it." His voice was shaking with laughter.

"In that case, you can bring me a cup too," she said, walking towards the staircase. She was dying to make love to him, keen for him to take away the hurt she had endured at his father's hands. But why had the wedding been cancelled? She did not understand. While it was an arranged match, it had been so obvious that Bhoomi and Roopak were truly attracted to each other; keen to become man and wife.

"Here." Mudit stepped inside his bedroom to hand her a mug of coffee before shutting the door firmly and locking it.

"Why was the wedding cancelled?" asked Dipika, sipping from her mug as she looked at him.

He shrugged. "For some ridiculous reason," he said, not quite meeting her eyes. "As I said, it's a long story. I'll tell you all about it later." Placing his empty coffee mug on the bedside table, he pulled his t-shirt up over his head.

Dipika put her own empty mug beside his, staring in awe at his magnificent torso when it came into view. "Oh man!" she said, waving a hand in front of her face as one would a fan. "Aren't you smoking hot!"

"You think so?" he asked, lifting an eyebrow as he closed the distance between them to stand right in front of her, toe to toe. Taking her hands and placing them on his chest, he took her face in both his hands. "Not as sizzling as you are." His voice was a gruff whisper as he leaned down to take her mouth in a scorching kiss.

Clothes flew in various directions as they undressed each other in a tearing rush before falling on the bed. Neither was interested in foreplay as he plunged into her wet centre greedily before pumping vigorously as they reached towards the pinnacle which came barely moments later. Taking deep and gasping breaths, they lay back on the bed, clinging to each other as if their whole lives depended on it.

Cuddled in Dipika's arms, his head against her breasts, Mudit was in the throes of sleep when his phone rang loudly in the silence of the bedroom.

Swearing violently, he bent down to pick up his jeans before pulling the phone from its pocket. Seeing Bhoomi's face on the screen, he switched on the call. "Bhoomi?"

"Mudit *Bhai!*" Her voice was bursting with excitement. "Roopak and I got married just now."

"What?" Mudit leaped from his lying position to sit down, wide awake now as a slow smile spread over his face. "When? Where? How?"

Bhoomi giggled joyfully. "Yes, five minutes ago, at the Ambika Niketan Mandir. And before you ask, we have only a few friends along with us here. I miss you, *Bhai*. And I'm sorry…"

"You shouldn't be, Bhoomi. And I'm so thrilled for you and Roopak. My hearty congratulations to you both. You did the right thing, getting married today itself. I'm proud of you, little one." Mudit was only being truthful, glad of the way things had turned out after the fiasco of the last week.

Dipika lifted herself on her elbow, listening unashamedly to the conversation Mudit was having with his sister. That much was obvious. She also realised Bhoomi had got married despite the fact that the wedding had been called off. How she wished Mudit had remained back in Surat instead of rushing back to Mumbai!

Mudit spoke briefly to Roopak, offering his best wishes before handing over the phone to Dipika. "Here, Bhoomi wants to speak to you."

"Bhoomi! Congratulations, my dear." There was a smile in Dipika's voice when she spoke to the newly married young lady.

"Thank you, Dipika. I don't know if Mudit *Bhai* had a chance to tell you how the wedding was cancelled and the reason for it. But Roopak and I decided we were not going to put up with the whims of our family members and went ahead and got married at a temple, with only a few best friends for company."

"That's truly amazing, Bhoomi. I'm so glad you decided to follow your heart. And I wish you both a wonderful married life together."

"Thank you, Dipika. I must say that it was you who inspired me; and will continue to do so, I am sure. I saw the way you stood up to my father the other day when he lectured you on tradition and culture. I remember so well how you said that it's important to let people follow their own dreams and aspirations; and how important it is to spread happiness. Following that, I realised I can never make my father happy, only because he loves to wallow in misery. First, he was sad that I was born a girl. Later, he was not happy because he said I wasn't beautiful enough. He didn't like it when my grades were poor. But then again when I did well, he did not want me to go for my higher studies, all because I am a woman. He insisted I get married. But cancelled my wedding after I fell in love with my fiancé." She paused for breath before continuing, "It finally struck me that my happiness cannot depend on another person, but only on myself. I called Roopak early this morning to ask him if he will marry me today itself in the same *muhurat*. And here we are, married." She laughed softly, bubbling with cheer.

Oh my God! Dipika was truly amazed by Bhoomi's words, feeling a tad emotional on the younger woman's behalf. "That's so awesome, Bhoomi. I'm so happy for you and Roopak, too. God bless you both."

"Roopak would like to talk to you, Dipika." Bhoomi handed the phone over to her brand-new husband.

"Hello, Dipika!" Roopak was grinning when he spoke to his oldest brother-in-law's partner, the woman he had met on the day of his engagement. "I don't know if you are aware of the huge role you have played in my life today. But for you, I wouldn't be married to the woman of my life. So, thank you a million times over."

Dipika was shell-shocked and went completely silent as she stared dazedly at Mudit.

Mudit reached over to take the phone from her nerveless fingers and spoke into it. "Hello Bhoomi."

"This is Roopak. I thought I was speaking to Dipika."

"You were. But she suddenly went silent and that's why I took the phone. What…?"

"Can you put the phone on speaker, Mudit?" asked Roopak politely.

"Sure. You are on speaker now," said Mudit, following his new brother-in-law's instruction.

"Dipika, can you hear me? Let me repeat myself. It was thanks to you that I tied the knot with Bhoomi today. I owe you one."

"I don't know what to say!" Dipika responded in a choked voice. Roopak's words were so endearing, as much as Bhoomi's words earlier. She could not believe that she had influenced the younger woman's decision today which had resulted in such happiness for the duo.

"I have a lot to say on the topic. This is how my Dipika is, a powerful and positive influence on those around her. Which is just one of the reasons I love her to the end of the earth and more," said Mudit in a passionate voice.

Bhoomi chimed in. "I hope you're going to marry Dipika and make her yours for life, Mudit *Bhai*, before someone else grabs her from right under your nose." Roopak had put Bhoomi's phone on speaker and all four were avidly listening to each other.

"Shh, young lady. You had better take off on your honeymoon while I plan my own life, okay?" Mudit refused to let on that his young sister's words had shaken him, well and truly. She was right, after all. What if someone did steal Dipika from right under his nose? After all, any man would be eager to make her his.

Roopak laughed out loud. "I know what you mean, Mudit. Bhoomi likes to organise people's lives for them, all the time."

Bhoomi protested loudly, even as the laughing Roopak shut the phone after saying his goodbye.

A red-faced Dipika who had drawn a bed-sheet around her naked form, turned to give Mudit a shy glance. "I still don't understand why the wedding was stopped. For all the trouble, Bhoomi did get married to Roopak in the same *muhurat*. But poor thing, there was no one from her family present there."

His sleep having disappeared with Bhoomi's fantastic news, Mudit sat up to lean against the heavily cushioned headboard before drawing Dipika between his outspread legs, his arms crossing around her front as she reclined against his massive chest.

"Let me tell you what happened after you left Surat…"

Thursday was the night of the *Sangeet*. Until then, Mudit had been to his home only for dinner every evening, that too, only because he did not want to upset his mother.

Earlier, on Tuesday, during dinner, Sharda turned to Mudit. "Where is Dipika? You should have brought her for dinner."

"She had to leave for Mumbai urgently."

"But… but why suddenly? I thought she was on holiday for the whole week." Before he could respond, she continued on an anxious note, "When is she coming back?"

Neither of them noticed Chandulal watching them keenly from the corner of his eyes. As for Bhoomi, she bent her head low as she pushed the *moong dal kichadi* around on her plate, her ears tuned to the dialogue between her brother and mother.

"She is not coming back," said Mudit.

Sharda was thoroughly disappointed, for two reasons. One was the obvious one. Who was going to help Bhoomi dress up for the functions? She turned to look at her silent daughter. "Do you know about this, Bhoomi? What are you going to do now?"

Without lifting her gaze from her plate, Bhoomi said, "Yes, Mamma. Dipika has already set up things with a properly trained beautician who is going to help me for all the four occasions."

"And you did not mention anything to me?" Sharda could not believe her ears.

Bhoomi shrugged. "I am still hoping that Dipika will return." She lifted her eyes to look directly at her father, her gaze accusing.

Mudit shook his head. "I don't think she is. There's someone who has come down from Europe to meet her. And the meetings might continue through this whole week."

"Is she that important, our Dipika?" Sharda was totally impressed. Imagine the westerners wanting a piece of her time! Which came to the second reason why she was upset about Dipika's absence. She had been hoping to pin down her son into agreeing to marry the young lady who had arrived as his partner. But that chance seemed to have slipped out of her control.

Chandulal lifted his gaze to his son's face, wondering if he was speaking the truth. Of course, Mudit probably believed it to be the truth. As for Chandulal himself, he knew it must be a lie which Dipika had told. After all, it had been he who had insisted that she leave his home, and Surat itself. He laughed to himself. What idiots! Especially his wife, for believing that the westerners were impressed with that Punjabi woman. Huh! He had no clue about the kind of contacts Dipika had. But then, he was like that frog living in the well, which had no clue about the mighty ocean.

Mudit smiled at his mother affectionately. "Yes, Mamma. These Europeans may or may not become her clients. But she already has many of those from all around the world, from America to Australia to South Africa."

Bhoomi's eyes went round as she finally lifted them from her plate to look at her brother. "Really, Mudit *Bhai*? I never knew that."

"That's because Dipika does not show off like some people do." The shot was at his father who did not bother to respond.

Two days later, during the *Sangeet*, there was a loud commotion when Roopak arrived along with his extended family. At his side was Suchita, his cousin. At twenty-three, she was a dark-eyed, voluptuous beauty with a shy smile.

"Don't you think she will make Mudit a perfect wife?" asked Chandulal, close to his wife's ear.

Sharda turned to give him a startled glance. "But Mudit likes Dipika," she protested.

"Huh! Just forget that Punjabi woman. She has no family values. Look at Suchita, the way she treats people with respect," he pointed as Suchita bent down to touch an elder's feet at her father's instigation.

Arvind, who had been standing next to Mudit, could not remove his gaze from the lovely vision's face. Oh my God! Was this the chick his father had been jabbering non-stop about? The perfect *sanskari chhokri* for Mudit? Turning to his older brother, he spoke quickly, "Tell me you love Dipika."

"Eh! Why do you care?" Mudit stared at his brother uncomprehendingly.

"Do you plan to marry her?" Arvind spoke urgently, taking a step forward towards Suchita, who was still too far down the crowded hall of their home.

"I think that's my business."

"Please, Mudit!" Arvind's voice was pleading by now. "Please tell me you will not marry the woman Pappa has chosen for you."

"What? Roopak's cousin? I'm not interested and I think I've told this to Pappa multiple times."

"Great, thanks." Arvind stopped in his tracks to hug his brother, kissing him on his cheek.

"Are you crazy?" asked Mudit, smiling despite himself as he hugged Arvind right back.

"I might be," said Arvind, giving him a grin. "I think I've fallen in love at first sight."

"Who's the lucky woman?" asked Mudit, slapping his brother on his shoulder. She was indeed lucky if she had Arvind's love.

"Suchita Kandoi," said Arvind in a soft whisper.

"What?" Mudit threw back his head and laughed, and laughed some more, inadvertently catching the gaze of Suchita's parents.

Soon, introductions were made. While Arvind was also drawn into the family circle, the focus was on Mudit as his name was the one Chandulal had presented to the Kandoi family as a suitable bridegroom for Suchita.

As for Suchita, just as she was lifting her head shyly to look towards Mudit, her gaze was snagged by a pair of dark brown eyes, belonging to a younger brother. Her heart beating like a drum, she stared into Arvind's eyes, unable to look away as she felt a powerful connection drawing her towards him.

During the *Sangeet*, she danced for him, her eyes never straying very far from Arvind's handsome face.

Arvind, who had practised his own dances for his sister's wedding, walked into the centre of the hall to fall in step with her, grinning from ear to ear. Neither of them heard nor cared about the conversations the elders were having. Nor did they speak a word to each other. It was their eyes which did all the talking, making promises to one another as they fell deeply in love.

Mudit made his stance clear that same night after all the guests had left. "I am not interested in marrying Suchita or anyone else you have chosen for me." His voice was firm as he faced his father, his hands on his hips as he looked down his hawk like nose at Chandulal.

"You cannot refuse, Mudit. Roopak is going to become the *jamai* of this house. We cannot refuse an alliance with his cousin. It will be a direct insult."

"Who set up the proposal? It was you, wasn't it?" asked Mudit, glaring at his father.

"How does it matter now?" Chandulal retorted, not quite meeting his son's sharp gaze.

Sharda looked from one to the other, an irritated expression on her face. It was obvious that Mudit was interested in Dipika and no one else. Why was his father trying to force his hand? "Listen, *Mudit na Pappa*. He is not interested and that is all there is to it. You…"

"That is not the end of it." Chandulal was shouting by now. "If we refuse, they might even cancel Roopak's marriage to Bhoomi. What will we do then?" he asked his wife, giving her a sly glance.

"That's utter nonsense, Pappa. And you well know it. If they try something like that, they have me to answer for."

"It is all very well for you to talk, Mudit. You will spoil relations with everyone here in Surat and then what? You will take off to Mumbai and will not return for another twenty years. It is the rest of us who will have to face the music."

"That was below the belt, Pappa. Even for you." Mudit spoke in a soft voice, holding back his rising temper with great difficulty. How dare he? As if he had chosen not to be home in the last two decades. Is that what his father had been telling everyone? Blaming Mudit for the estrangement with his family?

If Arvind had been downstairs, the argument would have been settled easily; once he declared his interest in Suchita. But he had gone upstairs, thrilled that he had managed to get Suchita's phone number. He was in his room, chatting her up even as his family members were arguing about Mudit's refusal to marry Roopak's cousin.

Mudit could have told his father that Arvind had fallen in love with Suchita. But it was not for him to divulge the information. And then again, he did not want his father's mind to work against that possible alliance, as Chandulal was renowned for his stubborn and rigid nature.

Mudit swiftly walked out of the house, stopping only when his mother followed him to the doorway and called out to him. "Mudit."

"*Ji*, Mamma." He looked over his shoulder to speak to her.

"I hope this is not going to stop you from coming over tomorrow for the *mehendi*."

Mudit laughed. "It's a ladies' function anyway, Mamma."

"But all the family will be here," she wailed.

"I will come. But only for you and Bhoomi, okay? And ask the old man to stay off my back. I will not marry that woman, not if they offer all their wealth and property on a platter."

His mother smiled at him. "I know. You like Dipika."

"You are right, Mamma. I do. I plan to ask her to marry me once I return to Mumbai."

She took his hands in hers. "I'm so glad to hear that. I only wish she was here. We could have celebrated your engagement."

Mudit pressed her hands affectionately, not saying anything. No, he would not have proposed marriage to Dipika, not here in Surat, with his family surrounding him. He would not have been comfortable, especially as he was not sure if Dipika would agree to his marriage proposal. "All in good time, Mamma. I am not in a hurry. And her work is extremely important to her."

"What will happen when you have children?" Sharda was seriously worried.

"Well, we won't cart our baby off to its grandparents; that much I can guarantee." The words slipped out of Mudit's lips of their own volition. He sighed when he saw the guilt on his mother's face. Well, that was just too bad. His parents had not thought about his feelings when they sent him away, had they? While the Gemini had made the effort to bridge the gap with his family, he still could not forget the way they had abandoned him as a child.

14

The *mehendi* ceremony had taken place without too many issues coming to the fore. While the women were busy having their hands and feet decorated with the green paste, Mudit spoke to Arvind. "Hey, listen. How serious are you about this Suchita woman?"

Arvind's gaze lit up when he heard Suchita's name. "Why do you ask?" He lifted an eyebrow at Mudit, not keen to reveal his feelings when Mudit refused to share much about his partner, the woman who had suddenly upped and left for Mumbai.

Mudit sighed. "Pappa is determined to marry me off to the woman. And…"

"No way." Arvind shook his head vigorously. "It's not going to happen."

"How do you know?" There was challenge in Mudit's stance as he glanced at the irate Arvind with an amused gaze. He was so relieved to hear the vehemence in his younger brother's voice as Arvind objected to a match between Mudit and Suchita. Good! No, better than good. It was great!

With a mutinous tilt to his square chin, he glared at Mudit. "Because I won't allow it. And also because Suchita will never agree to marry you."

"Am I glad to hear that!" Mudit slapped his younger brother on his back. "So, why don't you put a whole lot of us out of our misery by telling Pappa what your intentions are?"

Arvind shook his head. "No, Mudit. It's too soon. We both need to understand each other better."

"Fair enough. But are you sure she is the one you want to marry? Or do you think you might change your mind sometime in the future?"

This time, Arvind shook his head vehemently. "No, no. She is the one for me. I will never change my mind, not in this life. Or even maybe the next half a dozen lives."

Mudit gently shook his brother by the shoulders. "Why don't you explain that to Pappa? Please, Arvind. He's eating my head off."

"What does it matter?" A frown pleated Arvind's eyebrows as he looked up at Mudit's face. "Why don't you tell him to fuck off?"

"You think I haven't tried doing that?"

"He cannot force you to marry her, not if you don't want it to happen." Arvind shrugged nonchalantly.

"That's true. But he's going on and on that the Kandois might cancel Bhoomi's marriage to Roopak." Mudit wanted to kick the whole Kandoi clan; as well as his own father.

"You don't believe that crap, do you? Come on, Mudit. He is just saying that to make you fall in with his wishes. Roopak and Bhoomi really like each other and are keen to marry. All the arrangements have been made. And as you can see, today is the third function and it is going so well. No one is going to be so stupid as to stop the wedding at this point in time."

"I hope you are right," said Mudit with a sigh.

"I know I'm right," responded Arvind, placing a hand on his brother's shoulder. "I think you should chill and just enjoy yourself."

"Enjoy?" Mudit frowned at Arvind. "You think I can do that with Pappa breathing down my neck every few minutes? And with Suchita's parents staring at me as if they are propitiating a God?"

"What?" Arvind burst out laughing. "Propitiating a God indeed! Don't be silly. How can they...?"

"Look at them right now and you will know what I'm talking about." Mudit bit the words through his tightly clamped teeth.

Arvind turned to look in the direction of Suchita's parents and his laughter disappeared. Mudit was not wrong. They were eyeing his brother as if they could not take their next breath without his consent. What the fuck! "Oh my God!"

"Exactly! Anyone would think that I am still that twelve-year-old whose life is run by his parents. Grr!" Mudit was beyond angry.

Arvind placed a pacifying hand on Mudit's shoulder. "Let me handle this, bro. You don't worry."

"What do you plan to do?"

"I'll speak to Suchita."

"Do that." Mudit gave him a relieved smile.

But it looked like Arvind could not do much about the situation. On Saturday, during the evening reception, a major war of words broke out between the

Trivedis and Kandois. Actually, it was only two people trading insults—Chandulal Trivedi and Suchita's father, Premlal Kandoi.

"Chandulal!" Premlal stopped Mudit's father in his tracks, placing a hand on his shoulder. "Did you speak to your son about the alliance we are planning? What is he saying?"

"I will need some more time, Premlal*ji*. Let us speak about this again next week." Chandulal did not meet the other man's gaze as he muttered the words. He was fed up of trying to persuade Mudit to agree to a marriage with Suchita. It looked like his son was as stubborn as a mule, if not worse. He had tried talking to him nicely—at least, that was what Chandulal believed—and had also tried shouting him down. Nothing had worked.

"What? How can you be so cool about it, Chandulal? We are discussing my daughter's life here. After you spoke to me about the alliance, the girl must be dreaming of marrying Mudit. Do you want me to tell her that it is not going to happen?" Premlal's voice had risen by many decibels as he glared at Bhoomi's father. What a wimp! How had his brother agreed to let his son marry this man's daughter?

"Listen, Premlal*ji*. You are being unreasonable here. I told you I will speak to Mudit again the coming week. Right now, we need to focus on Roopak and Bhoomi's wedding. So…"

"Oh oh! Is that how it is? It is *your* daughter's wedding which is important, not my daughter's, right? What will you do if I stop the marriage tomorrow?" Premlal spoke in a threatening voice, glowering down at the shorter Chandulal.

Hearing the raised voices, people had begun to gather around the two of them, listening avidly to the heated dialogue.

"How dare you speak to me so disrespectfully? How dare you?" Chandulal, who was renowned for his bad temper, shouted louder than Roopak's uncle. "Just because you belong to the groom's side, it does not mean that you have some kind of power over me, do you understand? Tomorrow, when my son agrees to wed your daughter, I will belong to the groom's side. Does that mean I can treat you contemptuously?" His eyes were red, like burning coals as he scowled deeply at the other man.

Soon, the five-hundred-odd guests who were yet to leave the wedding hall after dinner, hung around to watch the free show, taking sides and shouting along with the two men.

Mudit and Arvind, and even Dinesh, who were at the back of the hall, drinking beer with a whole lot of youngsters, had no clue about the argument which had ensued. Roopak and Bhoomi, who were sitting not too far from the youngsters, were in their own world, chatting with each other, holding hands.

Sharda came there half an hour later, tears pouring down her cheeks. "Bhoomi, Mudit, come here. I don't know what to say, what to do. They have cancelled the wedding tomorrow," she wailed.

"And that's how the idiots called off the marriage." Mudit stroked her flat abdomen as he spoke to Dipika, his gaze far off as he recalled the drama that night. "Nothing Roopak said would change his uncle's mind as the man insisted that he was insulted and would have nothing to do with Chandulal Trivedi or any of his family members. It was a damn shame, you know."

"What did Arvind say?" asked Dipika, turning to look at Mudit's face.

"What was there for him to say? It's going to be another uphill task if he still plans to make Suchita his wife."

"One thing though. Kudos to Bhoomi indeed! She's a smart girl, going after what she wants. I'm so glad she took the step to call Roopak."

"I know," smiled Mudit. "Smart kid indeed." Before he could speak further, his phone rang again. It was Arvind. "Hey Arvind! Do you know?"

"Know what?" asked Arvind.

"Bhoomi and Roopak got married this morning."

"Whaaaaatttt?! This is so damn cool. But firstly, I have something to tell you, bro."

"Go on."

"Um… er… Suchita and I realised that our parents might never agree to a match between us. And so…" he paused, wondering about how to continue.

"And so?" Mudit's eyes crinkled with amusement when he encouraged his brother to continue talking.

"We got married too, at the Mahadev Temple in Athwa. We…"

Mudit burst out laughing when he heard his brother's confession, stopping him from speaking further. "Oh my God! Two of my siblings got married today. I can't believe this."

"Hahaha! I hope you aren't angry," said Arvind.

"Why would I be? First of all, let me congratulate you and your wife. I wish you the very best, bro."

"The other day, when you asked me to speak my mind to Pappa, I did not have the guts to do it. I thought I can become a hero in his eyes by accepting Suchita's hand after you refused her. But then, he never gave me the chance, picking up a fight with her father, carrying on until Bhoomi's wedding was cancelled. And oh, I forgot to ask. Did they marry at the wedding hall? I'm sorry I missed it. Did you attend the wedding?"

Mudit laughed long and loud. "No, no. The arranged wedding was called off. You know that. I am already in Mumbai. But smart Bhoomi called Roopak early this morning and they both tied the knot in some Devi temple in Surat itself."

"Oh my God! This is simply too much, Mudit. What idiots we have for parents!" Arvind was laughing his head off.

They chatted for a few more minutes before Mudit said, "Tell me if you need any kind of help. Pappa might not let you inside his home. But that doesn't matter. I can help you with the situation if you need to buy a flat. Or anything else; you name it." Mudit had enough wealth to buy half a dozen apartments in a metropolis like Mumbai, let alone in a smaller city like Surat.

"Do you mean it, Mudit? But I will accept only a loan, you understand? I don't want to sponge on you."

"Don't be an idiot, Arvind. Let me gift you a 3BHK apartment in Surat. You get to choose the place. It's my wedding gift to you and Suchita. You don't know how glad I am that she's my sister-in-law now."

"Hehe! So am I! There was a time I feared that she might like you more."

"No way," said his new wife, punching Arvind gently on his shoulder as she smiled at him.

"Listen, I need to go. I'll catch you soon. Bye, Mudit."

Mudit hugged Dipika, laughing for a long time. "Two down, two to go," he told her.

"I don't understand." Dipika lifted her gaze once again to his, so glad to see the happiness on his face.

"Two Trivedis got married this morning. Dinesh is kind of young and hasn't yet fallen in love. That leaves only me, for now."

Dipika locked gaze with the man she loved, her eyes asking him a question. After all, she did not want to misinterpret his words; not the way her heart was jumping into her throat, and her head buzzing as it tried to push her into assuming things which may or may not be true. Okay, he had declared that he loved her. But even then, it did not mean that he wanted to marry her; spend the rest of his life with her.

Mudit felt the tug of the Libra's Flame on his aura, as it wrapped itself around him, slowly and steadily, enveloping him in its warmth. Turning her around in his arms to sit facing him, he pulled her against his chest. Taking her chin in his hand, he looked deeply into her glowing brown gaze. "I love you, Dippy; and I would like to spend the rest of my life with you. The past week has taught me something: that I cannot live without you. Will you marry me, babe?"

Dipika smiled through the tears which filmed over her eyes, refusing to close them as she stared into his steamy gaze. "I love you too, my sweetheart. I don't want to live my life without you in it, either. And yes, I will marry you."

He leaned down to capture her mouth in a deep kiss, which was a promise in itself, of a future together.

Finally, it was the oldest Trivedi son who did the decent thing and got married in a formal Gujarati ceremony which took place in Mumbai, a month later, with all his family attending it. Dipika did not think twice before forgiving her father-in-law. After all, he was an old man who held no power over her. As for her own husband, well, Mudit was a Gemini who liked to 'live and let live', which suited the peace-loving Libra only too well.

"So, Ms. Dipika Sanyal Trivedi, are you happy?" Mudit held his new bride in his arms, his grey gaze glowing with love as he looked down into her beautiful face.

"Absolutely, yes. How about you?" she asked her bridegroom in turn. It was the day after their wedding and they were in the honeymoon suite at Rose Garden International, a five-star hotel in Ooty.

"I've never been happier in my life," he said, pressing his lips to the pulse beating at her throat. "Thank you, babe."

Her pulse racing as she felt the trace of his tongue over it, Dipika threw her arms around his neck and pulled him closer. "Make love to me."

"With pleasure."

THE END

REFERENCES

1. https://www.docdroid.net
2. http://sunsignsbylindagoodman.blogspot.in
3. http://www.astro.com
4. https://www.self.com
5. http://horoscopes.lovetoknow.com

Bibliography
1. *Love Signs* by Linda Goodman

OTHER BOOKS
BY
SUNDARI
VENKATRAMAN

SCORPIO SUPERSTAR
(Written in the Stars Book 1)

Kollywood superstar Chandrakanth, also known as CK, is a true-blue Scorpio, communicating with his eyes and believing in showing more than telling.

His website and social media consultant Ranjini is a Piscean through and through, fiercely independent.

It is love at first glance for Chandrakanth when he meets Ranjini; so strong are his feelings that he proposes marriage on their second meeting. Ranjini, fascinated by his starry persona, gets swept off her feet. The two get married without much of the world knowing—including CK's aunt and his ex.

The two women set out to settle their scores on Ranjini who suddenly begins to feel a strain in her fairy tale marriage.

While passion reigns on the one hand, there's trouble in paradise on the other. Although CK is by her side, the Scorpio in him expects her to trust him implicitly. But can the Pisces in Ranjini accept him at his word?

LEO'S DESIRE
(Written in the Stars Book 2)

Twenty-four going on twenty-five, Nishaan Ahuja refuses to take life seriously. Intelligent and highly educated, he's slotted to become the Vice President of his father's multi-billion-rupee construction business. Only, the Leo man wants to live on his own terms. He takes the identity of Shaan and goes to work as a farm manager.

Chaahat finds a quick-fix cure to her plumpness as she's desperate to become a fashion model despite her parents' objections. The Aries woman is stubborn, determined and fiercely competitive. There's a hitch though. Her body refuses to cooperate as she continues to abuse it and she finds herself on the brink of a physical breakdown.

The Lion is a know-it-all and has to impart advice. Will the Lamb realise that it's all for her best?

Sparks fly in their love-hate relationship as Chaahat struggles to achieve her dreams with a lot of unsolicited help from Nishaan. Will the lovers be able to get together on their own terms, what with the distance which separates them; and their mammas doing their utmost to run interference?

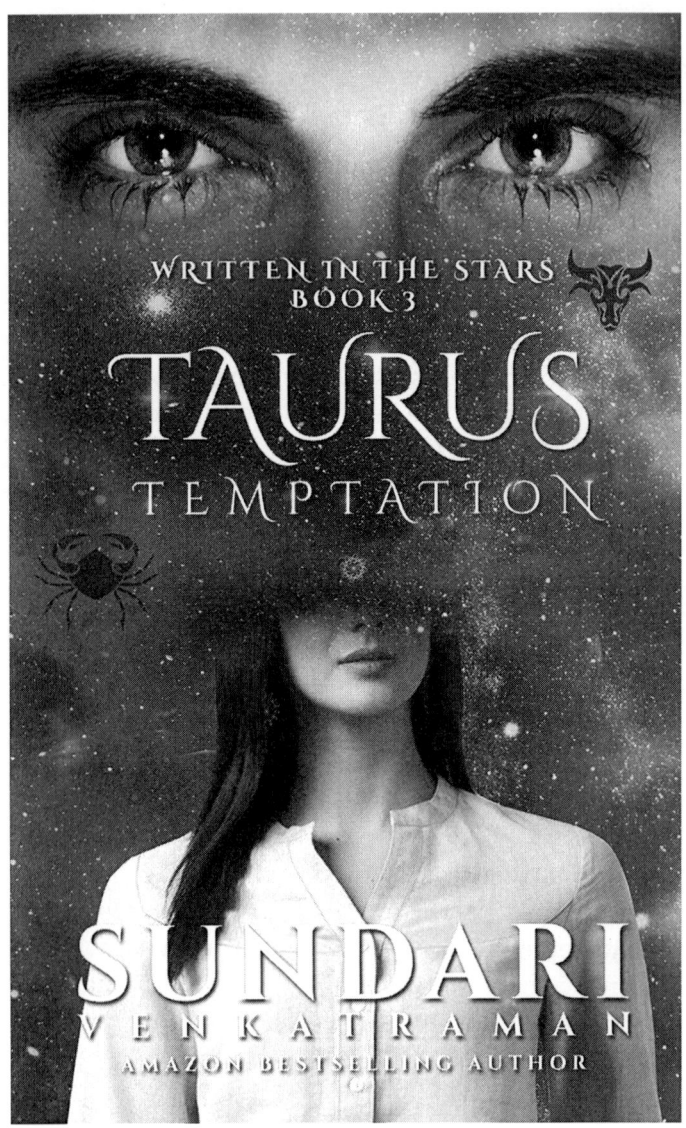

TAURUS TEMPTATION
(Written in the Stars Book 3)

Vidyut has a broken engagement behind him. But being the typical Taurus he is, he is unfazed when his fiancée from the arranged match hands his ring back to him.

Into his life walks Haasini, a successful entrepreneur in her own right. The Cancer woman brings a powerful dose of *joie de vivre* into the serious bull's hardworking life.

While the café owner struggles not to fall for the beautiful young lady, all because she is eight years his junior, Vidyut is unable to help himself when his heart refuses to listen to his logical mind. While Haasini has no qualms about admitting her feelings for him.

Just when things seem to fall in place for the couple, trouble brews from unexpected quarters, tearing them apart as it brings to the fore the jealous nature of the Cancer. While the bull moos loudly, the crab attempts to scuttle away.

Read the book to find out if they will ever find the happiness Destiny is keen to bring to the Taurus man and Cancer woman.

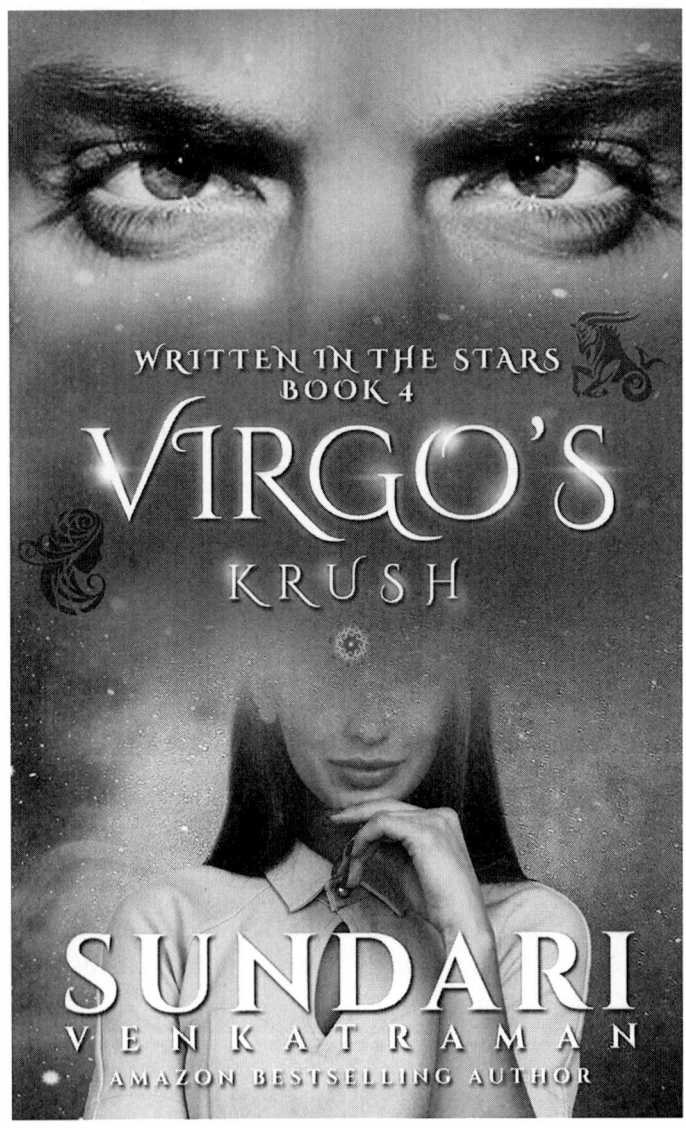

VIRGO'S KRUSH
(Written in the Stars Book 4)

The gorgeous and intelligent Sanjana is a fiercely independent Virgo. Or is it only a front for the woman who wants to be loved?

As for Krish, the handsome and internationally famous photographer, is stunned to discover he is father to the two-month-old Kabir. Typically aware of his responsibilities, the Capricorn offers to marry the mother who he is deeply attracted to.

But the Virgo, already crushing on the Capricorn, wants all or nothing and refuses to settle for a loveless marriage.

He pushes, she resists…

It's like the proverbial Irresistible Force meeting the Immovable Object…

Shall the twain ever meet?

AQUARIUS REBEL
(Written in the Stars #6)

Yoga instructor Shreya Udhas from Durban isn't at all interested in getting married, not when she's barely twenty-two. The Aquarius, who does not like conflict, is unable to stop her mother from going bridegroom hunting when they are holidaying in Delhi for a couple of months.

Chirag Bhatia runs an ad agency and is based in Delhi. The youngest of three siblings, the commitment-phobic Sagittarius is happy to let his older sisters provide the grandchildren for his parents to play with, while he himself prefers to lead the life of a fun-loving bachelor.

Sparks strike when they meet each other for the first time. And it isn't long before the Sagittarius guy and Aquarius gal enter a rocking affair. They don't even let the distance cramp their style over the next four years.

Until one day, Chirag receives Shreya's wedding invitation, to someone else. Shocked out of his wits, he's finally ready to admit to himself that he might be in love. But what if it is too late?

Connect with Sundari Venkatraman here:

- Sundari Venkatraman Books
- Sundari Venkatraman Books
- https://www.sundarivenkatraman.in
- Author Sundari Venkatraman
- @sundarivenkat
- @sundarivenkatraman
- sundarivenkat@gmail.com